His eyes were narrowed as they raked her face

"You think it's a joke?" he said with a hint of the grimness he'd shown just now in the gallery. "It won't be a joke when you've married the man and are trying to get a divorce six months later!"

"I don't believe in divorce."

"That's all the more reason to open those beautiful black eyes, Geraldine. Take a good look at your future. Do you fancy spending the rest of your life suffocating?"

"That's a horrible thing to say! Stuart does not suffocate me."

"Wake up, Geraldine. You were made for love—burning, glorious love—not a lifetime of being Mrs. Stuart Horwood, with a chain round your neck and a lump of ice in your bed."

Dear Reader,

We know from your letters that many of you enjoy traveling to foreign locations—especially from the comfort of your favorite chair. Well, sit back, put your feet up and let Harlequin Presents take you on a yearlong tour of Europe. **Postcards from Europe** features a special title every month, set in one of your favorite European countries, written by one of your favorite Harlequin Presents authors. This month, let us take you to Belgium. Join us as we discover the lovely city of Bruges, famous for its delicate lace-making and luscious chocolates!

The Editors

P.S. Don't miss the fascinating facts we've compiled about Belgium. You'll find them at the end of the story.

HARLEQUIN PRESENTS

Postcards from Europe

1619–THE ALPHA MAN, Kay Thorpe
1628–MASK OF DECEPTION, Sara Wood
1636–DESIGNED TO ANNOY, Elizabeth Oldfield
1644–DARK SUNLIGHT, Patricia Wilson

MADELEINE KER

The Bruges Engagement

Harlequin Books

TORONTO • NEW YORK • LONDON
AMSTERDAM • PARIS • SYDNEY • HAMBURG
STOCKHOLM • ATHENS • TOKYO • MILAN
MADRID • WARSAW • BUDAPEST • AUCKLAND

ISBN 0-373-11650-0

THE BRUGES ENGAGEMENT

This edition published by arrangement with Harlequin Enterprises B. V.

Printed in U.S.A.

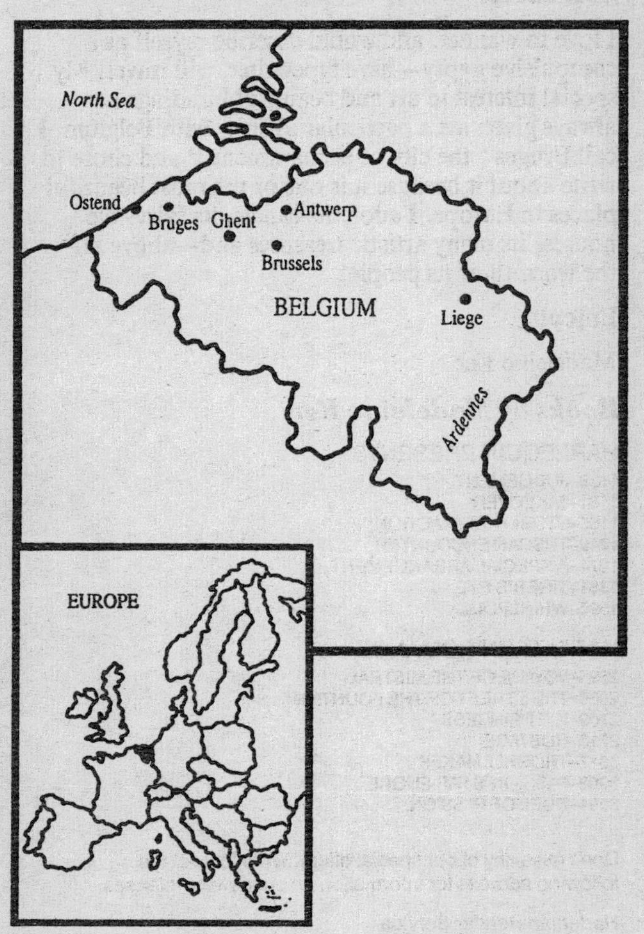
North Sea
Ostend
Bruges
Ghent
Antwerp
Brussels
BELGIUM
Liege
Ardennes
EUROPE

Dear Reader,

I love to wander, and would describe myself as a compulsive gypsy—have typewriter, will travel! My special interest in art and beautiful buildings has always given me a particular affinity with Belgium. I call Bruges "the city of enchantment," and chose to write about it because it is one of the most beautiful places in Europe. I adore its canals, its fairy-tale houses, its many artistic treasures and—above all—the warmth of its people.

Enjoy!

Madeleine Ker

Books by Madeleine Ker

HARLEQUIN PRESENTS

1138–JUDGEMENT
1161–TAKEOVER
1185–STORMY ATTRACTION
1249–TUSCAN ENCOUNTER
1274–A SPECIAL ARRANGEMENT
1361–TIGER'S EYE
1590–WHIRLPOOL

HARLEQUIN ROMANCE

2595–VOYAGE OF THE MISTRAL
2636–THE STREET OF THE FOUNTAIN
2709–ICE PRINCESS
2716–HOSTAGE
3017–TROUBLEMAKER
3063–PASSION'S FAR SHORE
3094–DUEL OF PASSION

CHAPTER ONE

STUART glanced out of the window of their taxi as it crossed the Grand Place.

'Of course,' he remarked, 'Jan Breydel is as familiar a name to the people of Bruges as Dick Whittington is to Londoners, or Peter Stuyvesant to New Yorkers. That's him up there.'

Geraldine Simpson followed his gaze. 'Which one?' she asked, seeing the two muscular bronze figures on top of the column.

'Not sure, actually,' Stuart said. 'Does it matter?'

'Who's the other man?'

'Pieter—er—Pieter somebody or other.'

'Who were they?'

'Ordinary men who fought heroically for Flemish independence in the fourteenth century.' Stuart Horwood had an encyclopedic knowledge of European history, and was undisputed master of little-known facts. 'Our Jan Breydel,' he added with a touch of dryness, 'claims to be a linear descendant of the hero on the plinth.'

She turned to watch the statue receding through the rear window of the taxi. The two men on their thick marble column had a magnificent setting. They stood at the centre of the main square of the Belgian city of Bruges, with its Gothic belfry, spired palaces and gable-fronted cafés.

'And that,' Stuart went on, 'is Breydel Street, leading down to the Prévôté.'

'I'm impressed,' Geraldine said, turning forward again.

'There are probably dozens of Jan Breydels in Belgium, all claiming to be Jan Breydel's descendant. But this is a very wealthy family we're dealing with, Geraldine. Top people in every respect. It's your first experience of dealing with clients at this level. You'll learn a lot. I just hope you won't. . .'

Geraldine smiled. 'I get the message. I won't let you down by spitting on the carpets, or drinking out of the finger-bowls. Tell me more about Jan Breydel.'

'*The* Jan Breydel or *our* Jan Breydel?'

'*Our* Jan Breydel, if you want to call him that.'

Stuart Horwood shrugged slightly. 'To tell the absolute truth, I don't know that much about him. He's young and forceful and runs a highly successful business in Brussels. A go-getter. Plenty of money, but obviously wants more. And, of course, he evidently doesn't have the slightest interest in Art.'

The last sentence was said with one of Stuart's disparaging expressions, a faintly lifted eyebrow. Geraldine smiled privately. Stuart Horwood was a cultural snob. In his book, Art always had a capital A. And 'not having the slightest interest in Art' ranked somewhere between stealing from alms-boxes and mugging old ladies.

She tried to imagine what Stuart's reaction would be if, like the Belgian Jan Breydel, he had been left an important art collection by a great-uncle. Sober delight? Discreet delirium? His options would certainly not include selling the whole collection off as soon as possible.

But then, Geraldine reflected, as one of the senior partners of Horwood & Littlejohn, fine art auctioneers of London, Stuart Horwood's whole life was built on art. It was more than his bread and butter. It was the very air he breathed.

Over the three years that she had been with Horwood & Littlejohn, she had seen Stuart Horwood go through many changes. When she'd first joined the firm, fresh out of college, he'd been nursing his invalid wife, Mary. She'd seen him go through the quiet grief of her death and the formal process of mourning that had followed over several months thereafter.

She'd always liked his quiet, dignified manner. And she'd always appreciated his thoughtfulness towards her. Some people had been kind enough to call her brilliant, but she *was* a junior employee, and Stuart's interest in her had been flattering. It had come as a surprise, but not as a shock, to realise that his interest in her was slowly but steadily growing into something warmer.

Geraldine Simpson was twenty-four. At forty-two, Stuart was exactly eighteen years older. And though her dark good looks and outgoing nature had brought her male admirers aplenty, she'd never contemplated a truly serious relationship before—let alone marriage, which was what Stuart Horwood had proposed eighteen months after his wife's death.

She'd turned him down, of course. As she had the second time. And the third.

In all, Stuart had proposed to her five more times over the past six months, until she'd finally——

Accepted? Said maybe? She herself wasn't quite sure what she had said. It had all happened at one of the discreet, quiet little restaurants that Stuart patronised. She'd been unwise to agree to brandy afterwards. It had been the brandy, she was sure, that was to blame. There had been so much of it in the huge balloon glass. Its fumes had stirred the confusion and affection in her heart into a muddled brew that had made her hesitate just so slightly when the by now familiar question had been popped.

She didn't remember having said yes.

But she definitely hadn't said no either.

Whatever she had said, it had made Stuart Horwood beam with quiet triumph. And what Stuart had said had been, 'You've made me a very happy man, darling.'

She'd been in a daze. Parked outside her flat in his Jaguar, later on, she had found herself whispering against his waistcoat, which smelled pleasantly of lavender, 'Yes, Stuart. Of *course* I care for you.'

Well, of course she did. Glancing at him now, she was struck by his distinguished appearance. His silvering hair caught the fine light of Bruges, and his grey eyes looked out with their usual calm intelligence at the city. He was a fine-looking man. Even her mother had been forced to admit that, though Geraldine winced when she remembered some of the other things her mother had said. . .

Well, Mother didn't have to marry him.

He might be a couple of decades older than her, but Geraldine had always enjoyed the company of older men. Not a father-fixation by any means. Just an appreciation for maturity, wisdom, and the quiet poise which Stuart had in such abundance. The thought of being Mrs Stuart Horwood, rich and respected, was far from unpleasant. Who needed a relationship of purple silk and blaring golden trumpets when you had maturity and calm wisdom?

'We need this sale,' Stuart said with a sudden hint of gloom. 'I hope things go well. This is one of the most important collections of art to come up for a long time. What with the recession, and the slump in the art market, the old firm could do with a nice, fat cash injection right now.'

'Do we stand a chance?' she asked.

'Well, he's asked us first, which is a good sign. But he'll also probably ask the bigger auction houses for their valuation, too. Especially if he doesn't like the prices we suggest. And you know that we never promise more than we think the market will stand. Conservatism has always been our watch-word.' Geraldine nodded. 'If he's the sort of man I think he is, he'll give the collection to the house which promises the biggest prices.'

'Whether they can get them or not.'

'Whether they can get them or not. Exactly. And then, we aren't the biggest or the most prestigious auctioneers. Not by a long chalk. It's going to be a problem,' he sighed.

'How will you solve it?'

'Two ideas occur to me. One is to remind Breydel of how good our contacts are with the Far Eastern buyers. They have real buying power at the moment, and if we can lure them to London we might get some healthy bidding. The other is to be flexible about our commission.'

She widened her eyes. 'You mean—take less?'

'God knows we can ill afford it,' he said. 'But that's what I do mean. Take a lot less.'

She was surprised. Over her three years with Horwood & Littlejohn, she'd learned that the auctioneers' commission was sacrosanct. It never varied. Stuart's suggestion that the firm might take considerably less than usual was an indication of just how badly business had been going lately.

There had been a vast boom in art prices for years, of course. But there were inevitable slumps, too. And this particular slump was a bad one. It had been going on a long time. Recent sales had been meagrely attended. Often, most of the lots had to be 'bought in' by the auctioneers themselves, or didn't even reach reserve.

Few owners of fine art were risking their investments in such a weak market. The news that the Breydel collection might be coming up for sale had sent a ripple of hope through the depressed art world.

And Horwood & Littlejohn had been delighted to be the first auctioneers invited to appraise the collection by its new owner.

'It's a notable collection,' she agreed, opening the folder in her lap. She read from the typed pages prepared by the secretary in London. 'Six early Van Goghs. Six Monets. Four Pissarros. A Corot. A Rembrandt. All these Flemish Primitives. *And* the prints and drawings. And this is only the stuff we know is there.'

'We won't get our hopes up about the Flemish Primitives,' Stuart said. 'Breydel is applying for permission to export those, but the Belgian government probably won't allow them to leave the country. They'll end up in a museum somewhere. However, there's no reason why the Impressionist works and the prints and drawings should be blocked. They might revive the whole art market. But we could be wasting our time and energy here.'

She laid her hand on his arm lightly. 'We'll do our best, Stu.'

'Yes,' he agreed. 'We'll do our best.'

Geraldine looked out of her window at the streets of Bruges, their quaint façades brightly lit in the autumn sunshine. She had a fine, oval face with a long nose that turned up at the tip, and large, liquid brown eyes. As a child, it had been charitably called an 'interesting' face. The nose had been too long, the mouth too solemn, the eyes too big. But as she'd emerged from her teens, all the features had grown magically together to give her real beauty. But for the impish glint in her eyes and the way the corners of her mouth lifted in a teasing smile, it might have been a Madonna face. As it was, it was exclusively. . . Geraldine.

She'd worn her hair—which was so dark a brown as to be almost black—at various lengths over different phases, from gleaming tresses to an Eton crop. Right now she wore it at what Stuart called 'half-mast', just brushing the nape of her neck, with a fringe that covered her high forehead. She was wearing a mulberry wool skirt with a silk blouse and a wool jacket, and carrying a large, sensible leather bag. She had a fine, tall figure, and in the elegant clothes she looked sleek and professional.

'Anyway,' she said, 'it's going to be a lovely break together.'

'This isn't a holiday, Geraldine,' he said reprovingly. 'The firm's financial health could depend on getting this collection to sell.'

'Right,' she said penitently. 'But Bruges is an absolutely enchanting city. And so quiet and peaceful.'

'Bruges is a well-organised city. Belgium's a well-organised country. The whole place is one huge art treasure.'

Geraldine nodded. It was one of life's little ironies, she reflected, that the Breydel collection had been left to a man who didn't 'have the slightest interest in art'.

'De Coninck,' Stuart said suddenly.

'What?'

'The man next to Jan Breydel on the statue. Pieter de Coninck was his name.'

'What a memory you have for details, Stuart,' she said admiringly.

The Breydel house was a gabled mansion dating from the sixteenth century. One of its ornate façades was reflected in a canal that lapped against its venerable red bricks. A high wall enclosed what looked to be a large garden at the side of the house, with huge trees whose branches hung tranquilly over the water.

'Nice place,' Stuart commented as the taxi let them out in the narrow medieval square outside the house.

'It's magnificent,' Geraldine said, awed.

'Jan Breydel's selling this, too,' he commented drily. He perched his grey felt hat carefully on his head, and straightened his coat. 'If you had a few spare million, it could be yours. Right. Best foot forward.'

'Best foot forward,' she repeated obediently.

They walked through the archway into a paved courtyard, lugging the bulky bags that contained Stuart's sophisticated camera equipment. The main entrance of the house was surmounted by a carved stone coat of arms with a Latin motto. On closer examination, the Breydel mansion showed signs of disrepair and neglect. The garden looked wild, and the ancient brickwork was in dire need of pointing in places. There was an air of desertion. When Stuart rang the bell, there was no sound, and Geraldine had the sudden thought that there might be nobody within. Nobody alive, that was. Just a few ghosts.

Geraldine was aware of a sudden thrill of excitement. The art collection they were about to see was a legend. Cornelius Breydel had been an eccentric but visionary collector. He had made most of his major purchases over sixty years earlier, when he'd been in his twenties. But he hadn't wanted to share—just to possess. Right up until his recent death at the age of eighty-eight, the treasures he'd bought had remained secluded in this great house, shut off to all but a very few privileged viewers.

Many of the works were known to the art world only in black and white illustrations half a century old. Old Cornelius had never allowed reproductions of any of the paintings in his hoard.

'It's a wonder this place has never been burgled,' Stuart muttered, ringing the bell again, and looking up at the high façade. 'You could get in here with a bent hairpin. The old man must have been——'

The door swung open suddenly, revealing a somewhat formidable-looking old woman in black. Her snow-white hair was pulled sharply away from a gaunt, distinguished face, like that of an old eagle. 'No need to pull the chain off the bell,' she said brusquely in English. 'Horwood & Littlejohn?'

'I am Stuart Horwood,' Stuart replied, sweeping off his hat. 'This is my colleague, Geraldine Simpson.'

'Miss or Mrs?' came the sharp response.

'Miss,' Geraldine supplied politely.

The eagle eyes raked her. 'You'd better come in,' she said shortly, standing aside.

An atmosphere of damp and darkness enveloped them as the door crashed shut. Geraldine looked around the vast hallway, seeing oak panelling recede into the gloom, and catching the faded gleam of some suits of armour and racks of archaic weapons. There was no sign of paintings in the hall.

The old woman was examining them both with no particular pleasure. 'I am the housekeeper,' she informed them. 'I have been instructed to welcome you.'

Stuart bowed. 'Delighted to make your acquaintance, *madame*. Mr Jan Breydel's letter mentioned——'

'*Mr* Jan Breydel,' she interrupted, with an acid emphasis on the title, 'is not here at present. He is in Brussels.'

'Ah,' said Stuart.

'He asks me to present his apologies. He hopes you will be quite comfortable, and begs you to proceed in any way you see fit. He will try and see you when his business interests permit him.'

'Ah,' said Stuart again, glancing at Geraldine. The old woman's words were polite enough. But her tone was biting, and her eyes gleamed harshly. Geraldine wondered whether that was her usual manner, or whether she had taken an unreasonable dislike to them, the way elderly people sometimes did.

She frowned suddenly, more aquiline than ever. 'Are these your only bags?' she asked sharply.

'Oh, no. This is just my camera equipment. Our luggage is at the hotel, of course.'

'Hotel?' The silvery eyes grew even colder. 'But you will be staying here, of course.'

'No, no.' Stuart smiled. 'We have booked quite comfortable rooms at the Hotel Adelphi——'

'I have prepared rooms for you here,' the old lady said.

'Well, that is really most kind, but——'

'I shall telephone the Hotel Adelphi,' she informed them, 'and tell them to send the bags round by taxi at once.' She turned and stalked off towards a telephone that stood on a small table.

'Well, really,' Stuart spluttered. He tapped his forehead at Geraldine and mouthed the words, 'mad as a hatter'. 'I say, *Madame*!'

The old woman turned. 'Yes?'

'There really is no need for any of this. It's quite unexpected, and absolutely unnecessary.'

'I have prepared rooms,' she repeated, in tones chilly enough to freeze Stuart's urbane smile right off his face. 'The linen will have to be washed in any case. Food has been bought. Fires have been lit. I was always taught that waste is a sin, Mr Horwood.'

Stuart swallowed, looking less composed than Geraldine had seen him in a long while. She nudged him. 'Well,' he said lamely, at last. 'It is most kind of you. I suppose it will be more convenient for our work to stay here a day or two, at least——'

'And will save you a considerable amount in hotel bills,' the old lady retorted. 'Bills which I hear Horwood & Littlejohn can ill afford to pay these days.' Geraldine saw a glint of malicious amusement in the old lady's eyes at Stuart's discomfiture.

'Yes, well—indeed,' he said, clearing his throat uncertainly. 'The art-dealing world *is* depressed these days.'

'I may be, as you say, as mad as a hatter, Mr Horwood,' she replied, 'but I have kept in touch with the art-dealing world for half a century and more. My name is Anna Breydel. I am Cornelius Breydel's niece. I have been keeper of the collection here for fifty-two years. Excuse me, would you?'

Geraldine was fighting hard to suppress a fit of the giggles. Stuart's cheeks had flushed crimson, and he was having difficulty swallowing. The old lady's hearing must be as sharp as a lynx's. And though her patrician face was unmoved, Geraldine felt sure a malicious cackle was echoing around the high, dark rafters of the hall.

But no wonder, Geraldine thought, she wore such an unwelcoming expression. The idea of selling off the treasures she had been chatelaine of for fifty-two years must fill her with impotent fury.

The call to the Adelphi took exactly thirty seconds. Anna Breydel turned to them as she replaced the receiver. 'First I shall show you to your rooms,' she informed them. 'You may refresh yourselves there. Then I will show you my uncle's collection.'

Geraldine was irresistibly reminded of a stern governess dealing with two grubby children in a nursery of fifty years ago. She smiled. 'That's most kind of you, Mrs Breydel,' she said, since Stuart still seemed to be tongue-tied.

'I am *Miss* Breydel,' came the quick retort. 'But I dislike the title. It is juvenile. You will call me Anna.'

It was an unappealing invitation.

They followed the ramrod-straight back up a flight of stairs and down a long corridor. Geraldine dared not look at Stuart in case her giggles rose to the surface again. But she could sense his chagrin and embarrassment in every step. There was nothing he hated more than bad manners, and he had been caught out in a way that must have acutely discomfited him.

Stuart's room was large, and—like the rest of the house—panelled in oak. It was sombre and slightly oppressive. The large four-poster bed seemed comfortable, however, and the leaded windows looked out over the canal. There was a washbasin in one corner, and a bathroom next door. In the big serpentine grate, a fire was crackling merrily. He would be grateful of that, Geraldine felt sure, when the autumn nights closed in on this draughty old palace.

Anna Breydel pointed to the basin. 'Wash your hands in that,' she commanded, as though to a small boy. Then she left him there to lead Geraldine on to her own room. With a last smile at Stuart, Geraldine hurried after her.

Her room seemed a long way from Stuart's. In fact, the old lady led her through so many corridors and hallways, and past so many suits of armour in unexpected niches, that she half-doubted she would ever find her way back again. The impression everywhere was of spartan cleanliness, but the great house was obviously quite unmodernised, and she wondered just how old the wiring and the plumbing were!

But at last their hostess threw open a door, and said, 'This is your room.'

'Oh, how lovely,' Geraldine said with spontaneous delight. Like Stuart's room, this one contained a high four-poster bed and a crackling fire. But if differed in almost every other respect. It was light and airy, and unmistakably feminine in tone. It felt cosy and snug. She went to the window and looked down into the walled garden below. The trees grew thick and green over lawns and flower-beds. Stone benches and tables had been tucked into secluded corners, and there was a small marble fountain which was not working. 'What a beautiful secret garden!'

'I hope you will be comfortable here, Miss Simpson,' the old lady said in her austere way.

'I shall be supremely comfortable, Miss——' She smiled. 'If I am to call you Anna, then you can hardly call me Miss Simpson. My name is Geraldine.'

Anna Breydel inclined her head fractionally.

'Please don't be offended by what Stuart said just now,' Geraldine went on. 'Stuart is one of the least rude men I know. He'll be mortified by his *faux pas*.'

'I have grown past the age of taking offence at silly boys,' Anna Breydel rejoined in her brusque way. Inwardly amused by the phrase 'silly boy' to describe dignified, staid Stuart, Geraldine was struck by the sudden thought that Anna Breydel's face must have once been very beautiful. Even in old age, the wintry lines were elegant and smooth. 'However,' the old lady went on, 'it is a phrase which has always struck me as peculiar. Though I speak seven languages, I am not always familiar with the idioms. Why, "as mad as a hatter"?'

'I believe it comes from the time when hatters used mercury,' she said gently. 'The fumes often affected their brains.'

'I see.'

'I do hope you're not insulted,' Geraldine said.

The silvery eyes held hers. 'You and that man—engaged?'

'Well, yes,' Geraldine said in surprise. 'Does it show?'

Anna indicated the small diamond that she wore on her wedding finger. 'That shows.'

'Oh. I see. Yes, we've been engaged for a couple of months.'

'He is a great deal older than you.'

'But I'm very fond of him,' Geraldine smiled.

'Yet you wanted to laugh when he embarrassed himself in the hall just now.'

The statement made Geraldine flush slightly. The

old lady's eyesight must be as damnably keen as her hearing! 'I have a terrible tendency to giggle at all the wrong moments,' she confessed.

'Then you are a silly girl,' came the characteristically swift reply. But the words didn't sting; and Geraldine felt that they hadn't been meant to.

'I suppose I am.'

'How old are you?'

'Twenty-four.'

'Are you competent?'

'I try to be. And I have Stuart to watch over me. I'll only be responsible for valuing the prints and drawings. That's my field. Stuart does the paintings.'

'Age has nothing to do with it, in any case,' the older woman said, dismissing her own question. 'Either you have the eye or you do not.'

Geraldine nodded. She looked round at the spotless room, noting the warm touches that had been added to make a guest feel welcome here—flowers on the dressing-table, a wool rug draped over a chair, a jug of water by the bed. 'I can see that you've been put to a great deal of work preparing our rooms,' Geraldine said. 'I'm most grateful.'

'There are servants,' Anna said shortly. 'I will see you downstairs in fifteen minutes.'

Unsmiling, she left Geraldine, and closed the door behind her.

Stuart was already downstairs, when Geraldine finally found her way, after several false leads, back to the main hall. He and Anna watched her lithe figure descend the staircase. Stuart had evidently recovered some of his poise, though his attitude towards Anna was distinctly wary. He had a large file tucked in a businesslike way under his arm.

'Ah,' he said. 'There you are, my dear.'

'My room's nicer than yours,' she told him cheerfully.

'How nice.' He smiled without humour. 'Perhaps we can begin now, Miss Breydel?'

Anna Breydel led them down a different set of corridors this time. So far, Geraldine reflected, she had not seen a single painting on the walls of this house. Nor any form of art, come to that, unless you could count the rather grim suits of armour as art. But when the old lady unlocked a door, and led them into a large, high-ceilinged room, she could not suppress a gasp.

The paintings were arranged almost haphazardly, all over the room. Some hung on the walls, crowded together. Others stood on easels, or lay in stacks, propped against the walls. Many were unframed. At least one had a large tear in it. Most were unrestored, and the older canvases were filmed with cloudy varnish. Her trained eye instantly recognized the vivid brush-work of Van Gogh, the lush colours of Monet, the exotic lines of Gauguin. But what a confusion!

'My God!' Stuart said involuntarily.

Geraldine knew he was exclaiming in horror at the apparently careless way these priceless treasures had been stored. But Anna Breydel took it as a sign of awe.

'One of the finest private collections in Europe,' she said with bleak satisfaction. 'All exactly as Cornelius bought them all those years ago.'

Stuart drew a breath. 'Do you have an exact catalogue, Miss Breydel?'

'No. Cornelius never wanted one. But that is what you are here for, is it not?'

Stuart and Geraldine looked at one another in silence. 'Well,' Stuart said helplessly, 'I suppose I'd better make a start right away.'

'I will show you the prints,' Anna said to Geraldine. 'Come this way.'

The old lady showed her into a small library down the corridor. The room was beautifully panelled, with handsome wood carvings supporting the shelves. It had lead-paned windows that looked out over the garden. At a first glance, the collection of leather-bound books on the shelves represented an antiquarian treasure in their own right.

In the centre of the library was a long trestle-table, piled with several large folders.

'The prints and drawings are in those folders,' Anna informed her.

Geraldine stared at them. They were piled thick. Dog-eared corners of old prints protruded from the manila covers. She noted a large coffee-stain on one.

Geraldine felt the same helplessness overcome her that had struck poor Stuart. 'No catalogue, I suppose?'

'No.'

She sighed. 'Well,' she said, echoing Stuart, 'I'd better make a start.' She sat at the trestle-table, and opened the first folder.

Lunch was served for the two art experts at one o'clock sharp. The food evidently had a long way to travel from the kitchen to the draughty old hall, lined with gleaming suits of chain-mail, where they ate, because all the dishes arrived cold. A mousy little maid waited on them, but Anna Breydel had retired, presumably to eat in more private—and no doubt cosier—surroundings.

'I think we'll suggest sandwiches and tea for our next meals,' Stuart said, studying his plateful of congealing lamb stew with ill-disguised distaste. 'Well. First impressions?'

Geraldine took a deep breath. 'First impressions are that this is going to take a long time. A *very* long time. You've never seen such a mess, Stuart. There are literally hundreds of prints or drawings in those folders. Some are labelled, but most aren't. And some are obviously *mis*-labelled.' She thought of the dusty chaos she had been wrestling with all morning in the library. 'Old Cornelius Breydel doesn't seem to have been a very systematic collector.'

'Systematic?' Stuart snorted. 'He was an old jack-daw. A hoarder. And that old witch of a niece doesn't seem to have been much better organised. Calls herself keeper of the collection!' He snorted, more loudly, and shook his head. 'Well, it's the same story with the paintings. A lot of them are unrestored, and, frankly, in very poor condition. That's a headache in itself. Moreover, there seem to be at least some dubious attributions. Two of the six Van Goghs are very doubtful. One of the Monets is an obvious forgery. The rest will need at least some cleaning before a definite judgement can be made. But owners don't like being told that their Van Goghs aren't genuine. It generally sends them into rages.'

'Oh, dear.'

They ate in silence for a while. 'Having said all that,' Stuart concluded at last, 'this is still an absolutely outstanding collection. It's worth millions of pounds. It would be the most important sale we've had in months. In *years*.' He pushed his plate away half finished. 'I desperately want this sale, Geraldine. I'm torn. Horwood & Littlejohn need this business badly, and yet I know that it will probably take weeks to sort the collection out, with no guarantee that Horwood's will get the sale at the end. Also, the problem's so large that I'm beginning to wonder whether we shouldn't call in some outside expertise.'

'An art historian?'

'Maybe.' He sat pondering as the little maid cleared the plates and brought on the pudding, a limp-looking fruit salad with custard. 'Thing is,' he said, 'we need to have words with Jan Breydel himself. It's no use him leaving it all up to us. He'll have to come down from Brussels and see the scale of the problem. Frankly, I'm amazed he seems to have so little interest in the collection. Anyway, we need a stronger commitment from him before we can invest several weeks in a cataloguing job. I'm going to get the old witch to call him after lunch.' He shivered. 'There's a terrible draught down my back. I'm sure I shall get a go of my rheumatism if I have to stay here a fortnight.'

'You'll have to wrap up warm, love,' she said kindly.

'I will,' Stuart nodded. He probed his plate gingerly.

'This custard's got a skin like a crocodile. And it tastes distinctly odd. Don't you think it tastes odd?'

'It tastes like custard,' she shrugged.

He threw his spoon down in disgust. 'If you ask me, this is pretty damned queer household.'

When lunch was over, Stuart conveyed his wish to speak to Jan Breydel to Anna. Her regal old face seemed to tighten even further, if that was possible.

'What is it you wish to know from Jan?' she asked grimly.

'Just some details about the collection,' Stuart hedged.

'I assure you, I am in a far better position to answer questions about the collection than he is. He is a very busy man, and he takes not the slightest interest in art—except in so far as it can be turned into capital,' she qualified bitingly. 'You're unlikely to get much further forward with him.'

'As I understand it,' Stuart said in a clipped voice, 'he *is* the owner of the collection at present.'

'Yes,' she agreed heavily. 'He is the owner.'

'Then it is to him that we wish to speak.'

Geraldine felt sorry for the old lady, despite her formidable manner. 'We understand that you have a great emotional attachment to the collection,' Geraldine put in gently. 'You've looked after it for fifty-two years. But we do need to speak to Mr Breydel to clarify some important issues.'

'I will call him,' the old lady said with clear distaste, 'if that is what you want.'

'It is,' Stuart said briskly.

She picked up the telephone and dialled. After a brief conversation in Flemish with what seemed to be a secretary at the other end, she replaced the receiver. 'Jan is busy right now. He will call back later this afternoon, when he has the time.'

'Fine,' Stuart said, rising. 'Then we'll get back to work. Oh, Miss Breydel. One other thing.'

'Yes?'

'Please don't bother laying on dinner for us tonight. We'll eat out in a restaurant.'

'As you please,' she said frostily.

'And for lunch tomorrow, a packet of sandwiches each will be quite sufficient. We'll eat them in the garden if it's fine. Cheese and tomato will be quite adequate.'

He took Geraldine's arm and led her off in a dignified manner.

On their way back to their respective tasks, he patted Geraldine's smooth cheek. 'I'm sorry I brought you to this house of horrors, darling. It's like something out of a Gothic novel.'

'I do keep expecting one of these suits of armour to jump out at me,' she smiled. 'But I wouldn't have missed it for worlds. I love this old place.'

'It wouldn't be so bad but for that unhelpful old shrew,' Stuart sighed. 'Why does she have to be so unpleasant?'

'You have to try and see it from her side,' Geraldine said compassionately. 'She's looked after this collection for half a century. It's been her life. To see Cornelius's brash young nephew come and sell it all off from under her nose must be an awful shock for her. Poor old thing.'

'Poor old thing, my foot,' Stuart snorted, unlocking the door of the gallery. 'Well, there's obviously no love lost between Anna and Jan. So I shall have no hesitation in making her one of the topics on the agenda when we meet.'

'What are you going to say?'

'I'm going to ask him to keep the obstructive old biddy off our backs,' Stuart said meaningfully.

It was two hours later, and the afternoon was already closing in, when Anna Breydel came into the library. Geraldine looked up with a smile from the pile of etchings she was cataloguing. 'There are some wonderful works of art here, Anna,' she said. 'These Dürer etchings are masterpieces.'

The aquiline face eased into the closest thing to a

smile Geraldine had yet seen from the housekeeper. 'Indeed,' she said drily. 'Jan is on the line from Brussels, Miss Simpson. Can you speak to him, please?'

'Oh,' Geraldine said, flustered. 'Call Stuart—he's the boss.'

'Mr Horwood appears to have left his post,' the old lady said, making it sound like a court-martial offence. 'The telephone is this way.'

Geraldine had no option but to follow the straight old back into a little study, where the telephone receiver lay waiting for her on a table. She picked it up with some trepidation.

'Hello? Mr Breydel?'

The voice that came down the line was deep and strong. 'This is Jan Breydel. Whom am I speaking to?'

'My name's Geraldine Simpson, Mr Breydel. I'm with Horwood & Littlejohn. Actually, it was Mr Horwood who called earlier, but he seems to have——'

'What is this about?' the deep voice cut in.

'Well, actually, we were rather hoping you might find the time to come down to Bruges to talk to us, Mr Breydel.'

'What for?'

'Well, we—er—feel we need to discuss one or two finer points with you.'

'Can't it be achieved down the telephone?' he asked brusquely.

'It would be better in person,' she said. She could feel Anna Breydel's silvery eyes fixed on her. 'There are a couple of problems that might arise.'

'I don't need extra problems right now,' Jan Breydel replied, and for the first time she caught the hint of an accent in the powerful voice. 'Is this a serious matter, Miss. . .?'

'Simpson,' she supplied. 'Yes, it is quite serious. I hate to impose on your valuable time, but the collection *is* worth several million pounds, and——'

'Yes, quite,' he cut in again. 'I'll do what I can.'

It took her a moment to realise that he had severed the connection. She found herself standing like a fool with the dead receiver pressed to her ear. She replaced it.

'Well?' Anna said.

'He says he'll try and come.'

'I know that,' Anna snorted. 'I meant *well*, what are these problems?'

'Purely administrative,' she said evasively.

'Do you still take me for a fool?' Anna said sharply.

Geraldine met the piercing eyes, and shook her head. 'No,' she said. 'A lot of the works need restoration, Anna. They're in poor condition. They're certainly in a confused order. And Stuart feels that at least some of the paintings are not. . .well, not what they purport to be.'

She braced herself for the icy retort that was sure to come. But Anna simply nodded. 'I see,' she said.

'You knew about the misattributions?'

'Cornelius was not always an objective man,' she replied obliquely. 'If it was signed Monet, to him it *was* a Monet.'

'Well, we have to speak to Mr Breydel as soon as possible. There's a great deal of work to be done, you see, and without what Stuart calls "a strong commitment" from the owner, we simply can't proceed.'

The older woman nodded again. 'If you need any help,' she said, 'I probably know the collection better than anyone alive.'

'That is very kind of you,' Geraldine said pleasantly. 'I do understand that this can't be easy for you. To see your lifetime's work broken up and sold off. . . I can only imagine how it must be hurting you.'

The old lady was silent for a long while. Then she gave an almost human sigh. 'The Breydels have always produced two kinds of men,' she said. 'The dreamers and the doers. Cornelius was a dreamer. His great-nephew, my second cousin Jan, is a doer. Cornelius built a monument to Art here. To Jan, this collection, this whole house, is nothing more than a heap of dusty old bones. He has his factories, his Ferraris, his blonde girlfriends, his nightclubs. He's impatient to shake off the past, and get on with his glittering new life.' She spoke with considerable bitterness. 'He is not the sort of man who understands things like tradition and culture. You will see that when you meet him.'

'As a matter of fact,' Geraldine smiled, 'I'm looking forward to that very much. You've just whetted my appetite. He sounds very glamorous. I don't know many dashing young entrepreneurs who drive Ferraris and collect blondes.'

Anna Breydel did not return the smile. She had unbent a moment ago, but now she was ramrod-straight again. Her gimlet eyes bored into Geraldine's. 'Jan Breydel is to women what a flame is to moths,' she said heavily. 'Don't flutter around him, Miss Simpson. You'll get your pretty little wings singed before you know where you are.'

And with that, Anna left Geraldine open-mouthed in the study.

CHAPTER TWO

GERALDINE awoke with a start. It was still dark outside, but something had roused her from her dreams.

She lay half asleep, thinking back over the evening before. It had been very pleasant. She and Stuart had hunted out a quaint little restaurant not far from the house, where they had eaten well and enjoyed each other's company over a good bottle of Rhine wine. They had walked along the canal hand-in-hand afterwards, discussing the prospects of the sale. They'd come back to the Breydel mansion well before eleven, and she had not heard the strokes of midnight on the great carillon of Bruges' famous belfry—she'd been fast asleep. She had dreamed of——

There! She heard it again. The unmistakable rattle of gravel being thrown against her window. She checked her bedside clock. It was four o'clock in the morning!

Mystified, but not really alarmed, she clambered out of bed, and padded barefoot to the window. She opened it cautiously, and peered out. She gave a little gasp as she saw the dark figure that stood in the garden down below.

'About time,' the figure said in an irritable mutter. 'I've been throwing stones at your window for ten minutes. Come down and let me in, will you?'

'You must be joking!' she exclaimed. 'Who on earth are you?'

'I'm Jan Breydel,' came the impatient retort. 'You spoke to me yesterday afternoon.'

'How do I know it's you?' she challenged.

'Don't be a damned fool,' he growled. 'Just let me in.'

'But—but—I hardly know my way around this place!'

'Go down to the kitchen,' he commanded, 'and open the back door. And get a move along, Miss Simpson. It's damned cold out here.'

She shut the window, and hunted for her slippers and dressing-gown in the flickering firelight. Her heart was pounding. Damn the man! Why did he have to arrive in the middle of the night? And why had he chosen *her* window?

The great house was ghostly in the darkness. The suits of armour seemed poised to spring out of their niches at her as she passed. That had been a joke earlier on, in the daylight. Right now, the thought made her hurry along, goose-bumps shivering across her skin. If she bumped into anyone down these creaking black corridors, she would scream her head off!

She groped her way down the staircase and along towards the area where their lunch had appeared from yesterday. She found the kitchen more by luck than design, and located the back door. It was locked and latched on the inside. She undid the fastenings, and swung the door open.

The man who entered was tall and broad, towering over her by at least a foot. He was wearing a coat and hat. 'You took your sweet time,' he said ungratefully, shutting the door behind him. He tossed his hat on to the kitchen table, hauled off his coat, and switched on the light.

Geraldine found herself blinking up at Jan Breydel. The first thing to strike her was the piercing blue eyes. They were the deep indigo of cornflowers, but there was no softness in their gaze, only emphatic strength of character and candid aggression. They bored into hers with a ruthless intelligence. His nose was hawked, along the same aquiline lines as Anna's. It surmounted a beautifully chiselled mouth and a strongly cleft chin. The bones of the face were undilutedly masculine, the jaw square, the cheekbones hard and vigorous. The hair that curled around his ears was a dark mahogany-brown. The crisp curls caught lighter glints.

He wore a beautifully cut dinner-jacket, complete with a bow-tie and a white silk scarf draped around his broad shoulders. He had the outstanding figure of an athlete, and did not look in the least like a man who worked behind a desk.

In short, Geraldine thought in a dazed way, no more magnificent male animal had ever appeared to her, in dreams or out of them. She gaped up at him, her dark hair tumbled around her flushed face, and couldn't find a word to say.

'They must make art experts young these days,' he commented, surveying the rest of her—plain white nightie and wool dressing-gown—with no apparent delight. 'How old are you?'

'Quite old enough,' she retorted, finding her tongue at last. 'How did you get into the garden?'

'Climbed over the wall, of course,' he rejoined. 'Did you think I fell from the sky? I don't have a key to this mouldering old pile, and I didn't want to raise my dear Cousin Anna—she's liable to snap my head off these days.'

'So you woke me up instead?' she said, folding her arms. 'Do you know what time it is?'

'You wanted to see me,' he reminded her, blue eyes glinting, 'not the other way round. I've just driven all the way down from Brussels——'

'Straight from a nightclub?' she suggested, glancing pointedly at his evening attire.

'Straight from the opera, as it happens. And I'm damned if I'm going to spend the night hunched up in a Ferrari outside my own house.' His English was near flawless, but once again she caught the harsh hint of an accent. 'Look, be an angel, and make me a cup of coffee, would you? It's freezing out there.'

Indignation rose in her. Did he think all women were chattels to jump to his bidding? But he had already turned away from her to hunt through the cupboards, and she thought better of her retort. This gorgeous, ill-mannered hunk of manhood *was* the owner of several million pounds' worth of Impressionist art—it would be wise to humour him a little!

She set about making coffee in the unfamiliar surroundings. The kitchen was as ancient as the rest of the house, but the kettle looked functional. Jan Breydel grunted with satisfaction as he laid out an assortment of odd finds—a jar of olives, some pickles, cheese and crackers, a tin of anchovies, a packet of chocolate biscuits. 'There,' he said. 'At least we can make a snack.'

'Is that what you usually eat at four in the morning?' she asked drily. 'Everything there's either acid or salty. You'll get nightmares.'

'I never get nightmares. Not even in this dump.' He reclined on a kitchen chair, stretched out his long legs, and studied her with those insolent blue eyes. 'Well, Miss Geraldine Simpson. You're not at all like your voice.'

'Oh?' she said aloofly.

'No. Your voice is cool and crisply ironed. Whereas in the flesh you are rather delightfully tousled. Rumpled, even.'

She gritted her teeth. 'What did you expect at four in the morning? A gold lamé evening gown?'

He grinned, showing beautiful white teeth. '*Touché*. I'm not very grateful, am I?'

She turned back to the kettle. 'How did you know which room I was in?'

'Saw the smoke coming from your chimney,' he said practically. 'I could have tried your Mr Horwood, but that would have involved swimming round the canal. I saw his chimney on the other side of the house.'

She made him the cup of coffee he had requested, and, on second thoughts, made a cup for herself. She sat opposite him, and watched him wolf down crackers, anchovies and cheese. He must be, she reckoned, between thirty and thirty-five. There were fine lines around the corners of his eyes, but that struck her as due to experience, rather than age. He positively glowed with health. He had strong, capable hands, with long and shapely fingers. Beneath the evening clothes, his body was evidently hard. He looked like an active man. Active—and highly successful. The watch she glimpsed under his cuff was a gold Piaget, and his cufflinks sparkled with diamonds. The clothes, of course, were the best money could buy.

He seemed to sense her eyes on him, and looked up. Geraldine flushed at the eye-contact. He had the most direct gaze she'd ever encountered. It seemed to cut right through her cosy dressing-gown and lay bare the flesh beneath.

'So,' he said. 'Tell me about these problems that have come up with the pictures.'

'That had better wait until working hours,' she replied primly. 'And Stu—Mr Horwood is the person to tell you about those.'

'But Stu—Mr Horwood is in his beddie-byes,' he said, mimicking her hesitation wickedly. 'And I don't have too much time to hang around tomorrow. I have a business to run in Brussels.'

'I know.'

'I'd like to get this whole matter settled as soon as possible,' he went on, polishing off the crackers. 'The quicker I can get shot of these paintings and this house, the better.'

'This place doesn't matter very much to you, does it?' she said. She'd spoken sharply, but his attitude had stung her. 'This house and the collection of art in it are less than the dust under your chariot wheels.'

'Very poetic,' he said, watching her through now-narrowed eyes.

'Your great-uncle spent a lifetime building up this collection. Now you're impatient to sell it off in a few weeks. Never mind all the love and hard work he put into it. Not to mention the feelings of your cousin.'

'Does Anna have feelings?' he enquired, tilting one eyebrow lazily upward. 'That comes as news to me.'

'Have you even looked at the collection since you inherited it?' she demanded.

'I saw it often enough as a child,' he drawled. 'I had

it rammed down my throat every Sunday. If you had any idea how I loathe this house and those mouldy old canvases, you wouldn't be subjecting me to silly—and I might add, impertinent—questions.'

Silenced, she gulped down her coffee and rose to her feet. 'I'm sure you can find yourself a bed,' she said, her tones matching Anna's for coldness. 'If you'll excuse me, I'm off to my own.'

'Mouldy old canvases', indeed. She marched to the door, but he had followed, swiftly and silently. His fingers bit into her arm before she could make her escape. He swung her round. She looked up mutinously into the splendid, hawk-like face. He was grinning.

'So even art experts have blood in their veins,' he said softly. 'Has anybody ever told you how lovely you are when you're angry, Geraldine?'

'That is so corny,' she retorted angrily, 'that it would make a cat laugh.'

'Or how your big black eyes sparkle so bewitchingly?' he went on in the same purring tone. 'Or how your cheeks blush so prettily, and that delicious soft mouth of yours tries to compress itself into a line?'

She jerked her arm out his grasp. 'Good*night*, Mr Breydel,' she said icily.

She hurried up the stairs, hitching her gown above her ankles. She was so angry that her blood was tingling. What an insolent, arrogant, swaggering man! What a cocksure, over-dressed, *vain* person——

Yet she could not stop herself from giggling as she let herself back into her room. She had given Jan Breydel a piece of her mind. And it was not unpleasant to have a man as attractive as that tell you that you were lovely.

Lovely. She clambered into bed, and pulled the covers up to her chin. What else had he said? That her big black eyes sparkled bewitchingly. That her cheeks blushed prettily. And that her mouth was soft and delicious.

Recollecting the words made her glow all over. She curled up and hugged her pillow. Stuff and nonsense, of course. All flannel, as her mother would have said. The sort of flattery men like Jan Breydel could spin out by the yard.

Still, flattery was undeniably pleasing to feminine sensibilities. And, as she drifted off to sleep, with a pair of vivid blue eyes burning in her memory, she rather wished that her own Stuart were a little more prone to flattery now and then. . .

She awoke again at eight the next morning, half wondering whether her midnight meeting with Jan Breydel had been a dream.

She lay in the four-poster bed with a delicious sense of being a princess in a fairy-tale. She looked sleepily up at the snowy white canopy, and relished the atmosphere of the old house. Somebody was whistling in the garden outside, and the big splash of sunlight on the wall promised that the day would be fine.

The master of the house was here. The thought of coming face to face with Jan Breydel in the daylight made her pulses quicken, and she sat up. He had definitely intrigued her!

Geraldine clambered out of bed, and caught sight of her own tousled reflection in the dressing-table mirror. With her flushed cheeks and bright eyes, she looked about sixteen years old. Was that how she had appeared to Jan last night? She pulled a face at herself, and wished she'd been wearing her best nightie and gown, the silk one with the peonies.

The sound of whistling continued in the garden. It occurred to her suddenly that whistling was a most incongruous sound to hear in this rather sombre old palace. She went to the window and looked out.

Jan was standing on the lawn, with one foot on the fountain, staring lazily around the garden. He was wearing denims and a black sweater, and his figure looked even more magnificent in the simple clothes than it had done last night.

He was really the most splendid male creature she'd ever seen. She looked down through the leaded panes at him, and reflected on Anna Breydel's warning. Moths and candles. Easy to believe. Nature cruelly equipped some men with every attribute needed to break female hearts; and this man had them all.

As she watched, she saw the silver-haired figure of Anna emerge from the house, and walk over to her cousin. He straightened and stopped whistling. She could not hear what they were saying to each other, but it was evident from Anna's stiffening pose that the words were not pleasant ones. She saw Jan shrug, and spread his hands. Anna moved as though she was going to slap his face. Geraldine winced, waiting for the action. It didn't come. Anna turned on her heel, and went back into the house. Jan watched her go, shaking his head slightly.

Then, as he had done last night, he seemed to sense Geraldine's eyes on him. He looked up, and, even over that distance, she felt the impact of those deep blue eyes. She moved back from the window as though his gaze had scalded her. What gave those eyes their power? Was it the extraordinary colour? Or the force of character of the man who looked through them?

She had showered, and was dressing—with rather more attention to detail than usual—when the knock at her door came. Her heart jolted at the absurd idea that it might be Jan Breydel again. She put shoes hastily on to her stockinged feet, and opened the door nervously.

It was Stuart, wearing a formal three-piece suit, and looking slightly irascible.

'Who were you expecting?' he asked drily, evidently noting her change of expression, 'your midnight caller?'

She kissed him on the cheek. 'So you've met Jan already. Isn't he amazing?'

'I've met too many men like Breydel to be amazed any more,' Stuart replied cynically. He shut the door, and put his hands on his hips. 'What *does* amaze me is your lack of judgement, Geraldine.'

'Why?' she asked, genuinely surprised. 'What have I done?'

'Surely,' her fiancé said heavily, 'even you realise the impropriety of gallivanting around a strange house at four in the morning with a man like Jan Breydel—in a revealing nightdress.'

'My nightdress is *not* revealing,' she said indignantly. 'Besides, I had my dressing-gown on!'

'Whatever you had on, you gave Breydel an eyeful of your charms,' Stuart snapped back. 'It's hardly pleasant to have a man like that complimenting me on my fiancée's—my fiancée's personal attributes!'

Geraldine saw Stuart's eyes drop to her breasts as he spluttered out the words. They were, indeed, full and high, and, though she'd never been so unrefined as to emphasise them by the clothes she wore, they had always provoked male attention. Had she really been improperly clad last night? she wondered doubtfully. Had her gown gaped open at some point to give Jan what Stuart called 'an eyeful' of her charms? Unlikely, she thought, dismissing the whole silly subject.

She turned away from Stuart, and began brushing her glossy hair in the mirror. 'Poor darling,' she said, smiling at Stuart's reflection. 'I'm sorry Jan was familiar about my personal attributes. That can't have been pleasant for you, and before breakfast, too. But if you know his type, then you ought to know that men like Jan are always talking about women that way. They can't help it.' She saw Stuart's grey eyes still filled with doubt, and put her hairbrush down. 'Stu,' she said, turning to him, 'if it makes you happy, I swear Jan didn't get so much as a peek at my attributes last night. They were safely bundled up, and, in any case, I only saw the man for ten minutes.'

'Long enough to make him a cup of coffee and a meal,' Stuart retorted, completely unmollified by her explanation. 'Why didn't you wake me? That's what you should have done.'

'It was four o'clock in the morning, she said patiently. 'I didn't want to rouse the whole household. I just let the man in out of the cold, made him a cup of coffee, and then went back to bed.'

Her fiancé was still frowning. 'Well, Geraldine, I have to repeat that you were very silly to get entangled——'

If Geraldine had a fault, it was a slightly shorter fuse than most people, with a volatile temper at the other end. Her dark eyes flashed, and a higher colour mounted into her cheeks.

'Stuart,' she said levelly, 'you're being a silly ass about this. If you don't trust me with every strange man who comes along, then perhaps you don't know as much about me as you think you do. Now, can we drop this subject? I find it very distasteful indeed.'

She went into her little bathroom, and shut the door behind her.

She applied lipstick in the bathroom mirror, studied the effect critically, then wiped it off, and selected a darker shade. With a male personality like Jan in the house, it would be safest to avoid looking conspicuous!

However, she was damned if she was going to look drab or inelegant. That word of Jan's—'rumpled'—still rankled in her mind. She applied her usual light touches of cosmetics with great care, and when she checked in the mirror, the face that looked back was beautiful, calm, and sophisticated. She was wearing her mulberry wool suit again, with a fresh silk blouse and a string of aritificial pearls, and the clothes suited her dark colouring to perfection.

This morning Jan Breydel was going to find that Geraldine Simpson could be every inch as cool and crisply-ironed as her telephone voice!

'Ha,' she muttered to her own image. 'The iceberg from Ealing meets the fiery Fleming.'

When she emerged again, Stuart was still in her bedroom. He was sitting on the bed, by now contrite.

'I was a rude old bear,' he apologised, rising and kissing her cheek. 'I had no right to talk to you like that. But the wretched man *did* say,' he couldn't help bursting out, 'that you had the most perfect breasts he'd ever seen!'

Geraldine felt her cheeks flush at the impertinence.

'I'm sure he's seen plenty,' she said, taking her fiancé's arm firmly. 'But he hasn't seen mine. Let's go and have breakfast.'

Breakfast was a very different affair from their rather dismal lunch of the day before. For one thing, both Jan and his second cousin Anna joined Stuart and Geraldine for the meal. For another, it was served right in the kitchen, so that the eggs and bacon arrived sizzling hot from the stove to their plates.

But the biggest difference was also the most subtle one. It was the change that had come over the whole household with Jan Breydel's arrival. The place felt warmer. Insane, Geraldine thought, but it was a real feeling. The staff moved briskly, with smiles on their faces, lights were on in the formerly dark passageways, and somewhere in the house light-hearted music was playing.

Only Anna Breydel, wearing her customary black, and with her silvery eyes cold as chips of ice, remained unchanged.

'This is more like it,' Jan Breydel said cheerfully, heaping bacon on to Geraldine's plate, ignoring her faint protests. 'Nothing like a proper breakfast. In Brussels, I usually start the day with a cup of black coffee and an ulcer tablet.'

'You don't look like a man with ulcers,' Geraldine ventured.

'Riddled with them,' he said, grinning at her. 'Stomach like a colander.'

'The day you get ulcers,' Anna said in her frosty way, 'I'll know the end has begun.'

'What exactly is it you do in Brussels?' Geraldine asked him.

'I have an engineering works in the city,' he replied. 'I manufacture components for various European automotive industries.' The brilliant blue eyes held hers with such intensity that she found she couldn't look away from him. 'Do you know what crankshafts, camshafts and flywheels are?'

'No,' she confessed.

'Nor do I,' he said with a humorous shrug. 'I can barely wire a plug. But they tell me that's what I manufacture. Does that answer your question?'

Jan Breydel didn't strike her as the sort of man to be ignorant of his own production-line, either; but she smiled, and went on with her breakfast. He was certainly not pompous about himself, and she liked that. In fact, she found his way of poking fun at himself rather endearing.

Stuart Horwood cleared his throat. 'If we can turn to the problem of the collection, Mr Breydel——'

'Not over breakfast, Horwood, for God's sake,' Jan said genially. He smiled at the little maid, making her giggle. 'Gertruida, put some more of that delicious bacon on Miss Simpson's plate. She needs feeding up.'

'Honestly,' Geraldine protested, 'I couldn't eat another thing.'

'You'll spoil the child's figure,' Anna Breydel agreed sombrely.

'Nonsense. A figure as magnificent as Miss Simpson's is unassailable. Plenty of bacon, Gertruida. And Gertruida, is there any of that home-made marmalade of yours?'

'I'll fetch it, Mr Jan,' the girl beamed.

Geraldine glanced at Stuart. This further carelessly admiring reference to her figure had made his face stiffen. He gave her a wooden look, as if blaming *her* for Jan Breydel's lack of taste!

Somewhat to her own surprise, Geraldine managed to eat all the extra food that Jan had ordered to be ladled on to her plate. Breakfast was her favourite meal of the day, and the light-hearted atmosphere that had arrived with Jan Breydel had stimulated her appetite notably.

'This place is damp,' Jan said, pouring them all more coffee. 'I've ordered the maids to make fires in all the grates this morning.'

'Jan!' Anna exclaimed. 'That's most extravagant!'

'We can afford a bit of coke, Anna. Great-Uncle Cornelius was too mean to install central heating, so we have to make do with open fires. It's nearly winter, you know. And we have guests. We don't want Mr Horwood and Miss Simpson getting creaky in their joints.'

'You were complaining of your rheumatism only yesterday, weren't you, Stuart?' Geraldine said. She'd meant to be solicitous. But Stuart's glance told her she had not said the right thing.

'I'm not decrepit yet, Geraldine,' he replied starchily. He turned to Jan. 'Mr Breydel, I don't want to insist. But I'm sure your time is valuable. So is ours. If we can get down to business. . .?'

'All right,' Jan said, glancing at him. He finished his coffee, and rose. 'Let's go and see these wretched bits of canvas.'

As the four of them walked to the gallery, Jan manoeuvred himself next to her, and took her arm in a firm, possessive grasp that allowed her of no escape. 'Are you sure you got enough to eat?' he asked solicitously.

'Quite sure,' she said, longing to escape. This would annoy Stu even further. But Jan Breydel was evidently one of those men who enjoyed showing gallantries to an attractive woman. He had drawn her so close that she felt her arm brush a muscular waist beneath the black sweater he wore. The contact was disturbing. It made her heart accelerate uncomfortably. The blue eyes were warm and intimate on hers. 'And is your bedroom warm enough? Bruges nights are cold in the autumn.'

'Quite warm enough,' she said, trying to squirm away. 'Thank you.'

They entered the gallery room. Stuart had rearranged the collection of a hundred or so paintings into three groups—the first containing the torn and the very dark canvases, including the Flemish primitives, a second group of canvases in good condition, and a third, smaller group of assorted pictures from the first two groups.

Jan took in the arrangement with one of his swift,

piercing glances. 'The Good, the Bad and the Ugly,' he commented. 'Well, Horwood? Give me the bad news first.'

'The bad news,' Stuart said, in his precise way, 'is that the third group of paintings—the ones I've put over there—are all of dubious attribution.'

'Fakes?' Jan said succinctly.

'I wouldn't go so far as to say that, exactly,' Stuart hedged. 'But the work of minor artists is often confused with the work of great artists. People who were influenced by Monet, for example, tended to paint in his style. Some later collectors have been fooled by the resemblance.'

'So that lot aren't worth the canvas they're painted on?'

Geraldine saw her fiancé hesitate. Jan Breydel's forthright way of putting things was not Stuart's style, and he was being rather put off his stride. 'Let's say that an independent valuation—apart from ours—would be helpful. But if my opinion is correct, then yes. The answer to your question is that these paintings are certainly not very valuable.'

Jan grunted. He stood with folded arms, his deep blue eyes moving between Stuart and Geraldine. 'So?'

Stuart straightened his jacket, a gesture Geraldine knew meant he was preparing for an uncomfortable interview. 'The unfortunate thing is that among the dubious attributions are two of the Van Goghs, one of the Monets, and one of the Pissarros.'

There was a pause. Jan Breydel shrugged. 'Throw them on the fire,' he said unemotionally.

Geraldine saw Stuart blink in astonishment. 'I beg your pardon?'

'If they're fakes, burn them,' Jan said with a hint of impatience.

'You don't seem to understand,' Stuart spluttered. 'This means a diminution in value of at least a couple of million pounds. And before we do *anything*, I suggest that another expert be called in to confirm my suspicions. Even then——'

Jan strode over to the third group of paintings. 'These are all quite recent purchases, aren't they?' he asked Anna.

She nodded. 'Cornelius bought most of them in the last ten years of his life.'

'When his eyesight was no longer so sharp as it was,' Jan said. He picked up one of the 'Van Goghs', a turgid canvas of a basket of potatoes. He raked it with a single penetrating glance that lasted a few seconds, then nodded. 'This definitely isn't Van Gogh,' he said decisively. 'The subject matter is right—exactly the sort of thing he painted in his Heunen period, around the mid-1880s. But the brushwork isn't Vincent's. Too crude and uninspired by far.' He raised a thick eyebrow at his elderly second cousin. 'Anna?'

'It's not Vincent,' she agreed shortly.

Jan picked up the other 'Van Gogh', and gave it the same intense scrutiny. 'The same with this one. The colours are too drab. Vincent Van Gogh could be sombre in his formative years, but he never painted with mud. As for this "Monet",' he added, turning to another canvas, 'you're right about that, too. The subject-matter is Monet's, but this is clearly a copy. In fact, I think I remember where the original is—in one of the smaller American galleries. In the mid-West, I think. This daub,' he concluded, flicking the frame with his fingernail, 'has no merit whatsoever.'

Geraldine was both impressed and amused. So the playboy Jan Breydel was not nearly as ignorant of art as he was supposed to be! That blazing glance of his had told him in seconds what it had taken Stuart several hours to patiently sift out.

Stuart was even more taken aback than she was. He cleared his throat. 'I'm glad you've seen the—er—nature of the problem, Mr Breydel.'

'Indeed.' Jan turned to his cousin. 'Anna, tell the maids to put this lot on the big fire in the salon.'

Geraldine expected the old lady to explode at this outrageous idea, but she simply nodded. 'Very well.'

'Mr Breydel!' Stuart said, and his emotion was such

that his voice had risen to a bleat. 'When I said that these canvases were valueless, I was talking comparatively! They could be worth thousands of pounds in their own right——'

'They're fakes,' Jan cut in pithily. 'I don't deal in fakes. More importantly, I don't want Cornelius's whole reputation to be tarnished by a very few pieces of bad judgement.'

That struck Geraldine as quite extraordinarily sensitive, coming from a man who professed to despise his great-uncle's achievement! She glanced at Anna, and saw an expression akin to satisfaction pass across the stern old face. She was evidently in accord with her cousin on this issue, at least.

'Now,' Jan went on, 'what's the next problem on the agenda?'

Stuart swallowed hard. 'The—er—next problem. Well, Mr Breydel, the next problem is all around you. The sheer scale of the collection. The days of work it will take to identify and catalogue all these paintings. The poor condition of many of the works. I've put all the worst ones in the first group. All of these need cleaning and restoration. It's a mammoth task, and I really feel that my colleague Miss Simpson and I cannot embark on it without a firm commitment from you that it's going to be worth our while.'

'You mean that I'll give the collection to you to sell?'

'Yes. That's what I mean.'

Jan stood, pinching his lower lip, thinking hard. 'What about the prints and drawings?' he asked Geraldine.

'The problem's even worse,' she admitted. 'It will take a long time to sort out what's what, and a lot of the prints need repair.'

The piercing eyes seem to stare right through her. 'I don't believe in restoring works of art,' he said after a short while. 'If they're damaged, then they can stay damaged. The new owners can do as they please. Cleaning is another matter. I know some excellent people right here in Bruges, who will come up to the house and tackle the worst of the canvases. But I can't promise you the entire collection, Horwood, until you give me a proper valuation.'

A look of distaste flitted over Stuart's thin mouth. Geraldine knew how he detested mercenary attitudes towards Art.

'I can give you that in a day or so,' Stuart promised.

'I'll give you my decision then,' Jan replied. He nodded to Anna. 'Anna? Speak to the maids about the fakes.'

Anna swept out of the gallery in her usual regal way.

Taking swift advantage of her absence, Stuart Horwood moved in. 'There is another problem, Mr Breydel,' he said smoothly.

'What's that?'

'Well, I hesitate to broach such a delicate topic. But the problem is actually your cousin.'

'Anna?'

'Yes. She's made it clear from the start that she disapproves of the whole sale, and in particular of our own presence here. She's been obstructive and unhelpful. I'd appreciate it if you could perhaps have a word with her. Ask her to keep out of our hair until the job is done.'

'Keep Anna out of your hair?' Jan repeated.

'Exactly,' Stuart said in satisfaction.

Geraldine was astonished to see the unfriendly expression that settled over Jan Breydel's splendidly handsome face. She could never have believed that those hot blue eyes could turn so icy cold.

'Let me tell you a little story,' Jan said, and she saw Stuart positively wilt under his gaze. 'A few years ago, burglars broke into this house one night, and tried to steal the collection. They were armed, four big, strong men. Anna drove them off with a poker. She chased them out of the house and into the garden, and they fled like sheep. She was sixty-six at the time.'

Stuart cleared his throat. 'My goodness.'

'Anna has guarded and maintained this collection for

over half a century, Mr Horwood. There is no one I trust more than her. *No one*. You understand?'

'Yes,' Stuart gulped.

'Good,' Jan said, his arctic expression easing back into good humour. 'She's not the easiest person in the world, I agree. But this *is* her home. Not yours. So perhaps the best approach would be for *you* to keep out of *her* hair until the job is done. Hmm?'

Stuart nodded without speaking. He had not realised, Geraldine thought, just how strong the bond was between Anna and her younger cousin. They might be in disagreement about many things, but Jan Breydel had just shown himself fiercely loyal to the old lady who ruled this house.

'I won't hold you up, Horwood. Carry on with the good work.' Jan turned to Geraldine. His face warmed even further. 'Now,' he said, 'while we leave your colleague to his labours, you can come and tell me about the prints and drawings, Geraldine.'

CHAPTER THREE

THE invitation had clearly not included Stuart, and Geraldine felt as though she were treading on eggs as Jan accompanied her to the library.

Being alone with him in the silent, oak-panelled room was not exactly a comfortable experience. She showed him the folders, and discussed her preliminary findings. She was trying to give him some idea of the scale of the task that faced her. But even as she spoke, she could feel his eyes dwelling on her face, her hands, her figure—and she was certain in her heart that he knew exactly what the scale of the task was, and that he was far more interested in her own feminine person than in the dusty heaps of etchings on the table!

'So you see,' she concluded, 'your great-uncle Cornelius had magnificent taste, but he wasn't a very methodical collector. He seems to have filed the prints and drawings according to his own tastes, rather than according to artist, period, or subject-matter. That gives me a big problem.'

She looked up. He was standing in what she'd come to know as a characteristic pose, with his sinewy arms folded across his chest. The way he was looking at her made her stomach suddenly turn over inside her. It was a very warm, very intimate gaze—as though he were doing things to her in his mind that had nothing to do with Art!

'Anna tells me,' he said softly, 'that you are engaged to that dry old stick. Is that really possible?'

She gaped like a goldfish, then found her voice. It did not come out as forcefully as she wanted it to, but she made a valiant effort. 'Yes,' she said, 'I am engaged to Stuart Horwood. But, considering that he can only be ten years older than you, you hardly have the right to call him a "dry old stick"!'

'Horwood was born a dry old stick,' Jan said. 'He must be twenty years older than you, Geraldine. That wouldn't matter, of course, if he weren't such a pompous little twerp.'

In her outrage, a succession of phrases jostled in her mind. *How dare you? Mind our own business! You have no right!* But they all sounded ridiculously Victorian in her own ears.

And while she was searching unsuccessfully for the right retort, what *did* rise to her lips was her disastrous old enemy—a fit of the giggles.

She tried to cover them with her palms, but they burst through nevertheless. She cursed herself roundly even as her shoulders shook. Why did the damned things always have to come up to the surface at the wrong moment?

It had been something about hearing Stuart—her boss and mentor and fiancé, the man she respected more than anyone except Dad—described as 'a pompous little twerp' that had set her off.

'You're impossible,' she said, getting control of herself. 'And you're a most abominably rude man. Stuart is a wonderful person.'

He was not sharing her amusement. His eyes were narrowed as they raked her face. 'You think it's a joke?' he said, with a hint of the grimness he'd shown just now in the gallery. 'It won't be a joke when you've married the man, and are trying to get a divorce six months later!'

'I don't believe in divorce,' she retorted.

'Nor do I. And that's all the more reason to open those beautiful black eyes, Geraldine. Take a good look at your future. Do you fancy spending the rest of your life suffocating?'

The word was cruel, and wiped the last of her giggles off her mouth. 'That's a horrible thing to say! Stuart does not suffocate me.'

'He will.' Jan moved closer to her, and took her arm. He shook her gently. 'Wake up, Geraldine. You were made for love—burning, glorious love—not a lifetime of being Mrs Stuart Horwood, with a chain round your neck, and a lump of ice in your bed.'

'Now look here,' she said, really starting to get annoyed, 'I don't know who on earth you think you are, Jan Breydel, but you have no business poking your nose into my life! I'm here to do a job, and not to be psychoanalysed by a womanising playboy——'

'A womanising playboy? Ah. Anna has been singing my praises to you, I see.'

'So you can stay out of my hair, and Stuart will stay out of Anna's hair, and we can all jolly well stay out of each other's hair until this job is done,' she concluded briskly, aware that her colour—as well as her temper—was up. 'You've already caused me no end of trouble this morning. How dare you suggest to Stuart that I appeared to you half naked last night?'

'All I said,' he purred, 'was that you have the most perfect breasts I've ever seen. I didn't say you were half naked. But your night-clothes cling to your body in a very seductive way, Geraldine, and I would have been less than human if I hadn't noticed your splendid curves.'

Somehow, having the man repeat his compliment to her in person was a lot more disturbing than hearing it relayed to her via Stuart—no matter how impertinent and unwelcome that compliment might be. She swallowed, finding that her mouth was suddenly dry. 'You were extremely mischievous to say what you did. I half suspect you deliberately wanted to upset Stuart!'

'You're right,' he agreed, 'I did!' He moved even closer to her. She tried to back away, but her retreat was blocked by the table behind her. One corner of it was now pressing into the backs of her thighs.

He took her hand, and lifted it, turning her engagement ring to the light. The small stone sparkled. 'Is this little thing the best he could afford?' he asked mockingly.

'It suits me fine,' she retorted, twisting her fingers fiercely out of his.

'He must have a mean streak.'

'Unlike some people, we don't believe in making a gaudy show. Besides,' she added, 'the art business isn't doing all that well lately.'

'So he isn't even a generous sugar-daddy,' Jan snorted. 'You really are on a losing streak, Geraldine!'

'Look here, Jan——'

'I'm looking,' he said softly. The closer he got, the more devastatingly handsome he appeared. He reached up and brushed the dark hair away from her face. Geraldine flinched as the gesture turned into a slow caress that trailed down her cheek and reached her mouth. 'I'm looking. And I see beauty. I repudiate the term "womaniser", he whispered, caressing her lips with as much tenderness as though they'd been rose-petals. 'But I do consider myself a connoisseur of women. And you are one of the loveliest creatures I have ever come across.'

'Mr Breydel—Jan——'

'Lovely. . .and spirited. Like an untamed Arabian mare. Fascinating. Entrancing.'

The eyes were drowning her in a hot blue ocean. She felt her senses swimming. She put her hand on his chest, meaning to push him firmly away. But somehow the feel of his hard muscles under her palm robbed her of strength. What had meant to be a shove turned into something a lot closer to. . .a caress. 'Please,' she said, in a husky voice that did not sound remotely like her own, 'don't be a pig, Jan. It isn't worthy of you.'

'You have no idea what is or isn't worthy of me,' he replied. He caressed her neck with his fingertips, studying her with hooded eyes as she shuddered in reaction. 'Men like Horwood always pick women like you,' he said. 'It's one of nature's little jokes. Pairing a beautiful, warm-blooded girl with a desiccated old mummy.'

'That's grossly unfair,' she choked. His caress was raising goose-bumps all over her body. She could feel every nerve tingle. As for the breasts that he admired so much, their centres had peaked into aching knots. 'Would you stop touching me, please?' she burst out.

He smiled lazily, then dropped his hand. But he did not step back, and she remained pinned against the edge of the table, a butterfly fluttering under the magnifying glass.

'I hope you realise,' he said, conversationally, 'that but for Stuart Horwood this meeting would be one of those magical moments that only come along once in a lifetime. My meeting you here, I mean.'

'Mr Breydel, this is one of those moments that come along with monotonous regularity in *my* life,' she said, trying to moisten her lips with her tongue. 'I often meet our clients while I'm valuing their work. And so far they've always managed to behave with a modicum of good manners. I just wish you would do the same!'

'I never conform to type.' He smiled. 'It's one of the qualities you'll come to appreciate in me over the years.'

'Over the years?' she repeated in disbelief. 'Mr Breydel, our acquaintance is not going to last above a couple of *weeks*. Furthermore,' she said, putting her hand on his chest, and this time summoning the strength to push him away, hard, 'if you don't stop looming over me like an iceberg looming over the *Titanic*, I'm going to ask Stuart to send me straight back to London, and replace me with our other prints expert, Miss Bridges, who is seventy-five, and has a mole on each cheek!'

She just had invented Miss Bridges on the spur of the moment, but the threat seemed to work where entreaties had not. Jan released her, and walked over to the window. She took a series of shaky breaths to try and calm her pounding heart. She felt exactly like the *Titanic* after its contact with the iceberg—holed below the water-line, and sinking steadily!

Jan turned to smile at her, his tall figure silhouetted against the leaded panes. 'You're adorable,' he said frankly. 'Absolutely adorable. But thoroughbreds need to be handled with gentleness. You have to be a gentleman to tame one. Tell me, Geraldine, have you any idea what a magnificent city Bruges is?'

'I haven't seen a lot of it so far,' she said guardedly.

'Well, promise you won't scuttle back to London, and I promise I'll show you one of Europe's most beautiful cities.'

'I'm here to do a job of work,' she retorted, 'not gallivant around Bruges with you!'

'You're here at my invitation,' he said softly. 'I'll leave you to your dusty old prints, Geraldine.'

He blew her a kiss, a graceful gesture that did nothing to soothe her ruffled emotions, and left her in the library.

She sank into a chair, and pulled her hair away from her cheek where Jan Breydel's caress had ruffled it. Her own palms were damp, and her stomach had never managed to turn itself the right way up again. In fact, it felt as though he had twisted it into knots.

She tried to concentrate on her work, but the black and white images blurred in front of her eyes, and the fine lines jumped as though she needed glasses—and she had twenty-twenty vision.

'You're adorable. Absolutely adorable.'

The words echoed in her head, distracting her like a swarm of buzzing bees.

It was not until she'd sneaked to the bathroom and rinsed her face and throat in cool water that she felt anywhere near composed again.

As it was, she started like a fallow deer when Jan Breydel came back into the library an hour or two later.

'What's all this nonsense about you and Horwood lunching off sandwiches in the garden?' he demanded.

'Well—er—we decided yesterday that we didn't want to disturb Anna unnecessarily.'

Jan snorted. 'The idea of feeding you on cheese and tomato sandwiches is absurd.'

'Cheese and tomato are Stuart's favourites,' she said practically.

'Not while I'm in the house,' he growled. 'We'll all eat in the kitchen, like a family. Hot food and good wine. Lunch is at one-fifteen sharp. I'll tell Horwood.'

* * *

Lunch was indeed served at one-fifteen sharp. And it was as hot as Jan had promised, and accompanied by an excellent red wine. Jan Breydel's presence, Geraldine couldn't help noticing again, had transformed this household from a spooky old ruin into a cheerfully functioning home.

As before, Jan did most of the talking. What he said was amusing and witty, and mostly directed at Geraldine. And as before, Anna and Stuart were largely silent. Anna looked her usual aquiline, reserved self. But Stuart, Geraldine could tell, was inwardly seething. He did *not* like Jan Breydel, and he definitely did not like the innumerable flattering attentions that Jan showed his fiancée.

At one point, when Jan reached out—apparently without noticing—and covered Geraldine's fingers with his own warm, possessive clasp, she saw Stuart's face clench in bitterness. She tried to pull her fingers out of Jan's, but he held on tight.

'I suppose,' he was saying genially, 'that I shall have to bite the bullet and stay on here another day or two, while you make your valuation, Horwood. I hate neglecting my work, but one must do one's duty. Hmm?'

'I'll try and have a figure for you by tomorrow lunchtime,' Stuart said through gritted teeth, eyeing the large, strong hand that held Geraldine's.

'Good man,' Jan smiled. His teeth were really superb. Had he spent several thousands on the best dentistry available, she wondered, or was he just perfectly endowed in every department?

She managed to disengage her fingers from Jan's at last. She turned to Anna. 'Anna—does that offer of help still hold?'

'Of course,' the old lady said, inclining her head.

'Then I'd very much appreciate it if you could give me a little advice in the library this afternoon. There are some things I'm not quite sure of.'

'I shall try to help,' Anna said in her customarily frosty way. But Geraldine thought she looked pleased to have been asked. And incidentally, she thought, Anna's presence in the library might keep Jan out of her hair this afternoon!

After complimenting the cook on the lunch Jan announced that he had telephone calls to make, and rose from the table.

Anna followed him a little while later. 'I'll come to the library at around three,' she told Geraldine. 'I'm accustomed to a short rest after lunch. I am no longer a young woman.'

'Of course,' Geraldine beamed.

She and Stuart were left alone. 'Well,' Stuart said heavily, looking up at her. 'What happened between you and that man in the library?'

'Why, nothing, of course,' she replied. But the flaming colour had leaped to her cheeks, and Stuart saw it.

'I don't often take dislikes to people,' Stuart said in what was, for him, a savage tone, 'but I've never met two people I liked less on first acquaintance than Anna and Jan Breydel!'

'Really? As a matter of fact, I quite like them both.' Geraldine smiled. 'They're real characters, both of them.'

'They belong in Madame Tussaud's,' was Stuart's comment. 'If the man interferes with your work in any way, Geraldine, tell me at once. I'll sort him out.'

'Thank you, Stu,' she said meekly, though she privately wondered just how Stuart was going to 'sort out' Jan Breydel.

'Can't wait to get this job done and get out of here,' Stuart muttered, pouring the last of the wine into his own glass. 'Hate this place. Hate this family. I'm even starting to hate old Cornelius Breydel. Inconsiderate old buzzard that he must have been.'

'He didn't create this collection for our benefit, Stu,' she said, laughing at his ill-humour.

'I reckon I can get my work done in a couple of weeks,' he said. 'And you?'

She calculated, then shook her head regretfully. 'No

way, I'm afraid. I'm going to need at least another week more, Stu, and maybe even longer.'

'Damn,' he said explosively.

She knew what he was thinking. 'Maybe he'll let us take the prints and drawings back to London?'

Stuart's answer was a snort.

'Well, if I do have to stay on here on my own, I'm quite capable of looking after myself. And I'll have Anna to chaperon me.'

'That's like asking an old she-wolf to chaperon a lamb against a tiger,' he rasped.

'Oh, Stu. I love it when you get all protective and huffy.'

'I'm not huffy. The man's a menace.'

'Didn't I tell you that I was a black belt in ju-jitsu?' She smiled, getting up and coming over to him. 'Don't worry, love. I'll be fine.' He allowed her to cuddle him, then pushed her away.

'Come on,' he ordered, scraping his chair back, 'let's get down to work. The sooner we're both home in London, the better I'll like it.'

On her way back to the library, Geraldine paused at a window. It looked out on to the courtyard by which they'd first entered the house. Parked on the flagstones outside was a Ferrari sports car. Jan's, without doubt.

The Ferrari was blood-red, and its glorious lines seemed to vibrate with life, as though it were trembling to take off, and roar away into a magical world of romance and excitement. She leaned on the sill and studied it wistfully, her chin cupped in her hands. The car was like the man—something out of a dream. Fantastic. Beautiful. But also dangerous. Liable to land you in a great deal of hot water. What had been Anna's phrase? 'You'll get your pretty little wings singed before you know where you are.' Well, that was clear enough.

Geraldine sighed, shook her head at the Ferrari, and went on her way.

As she sorted through the apparently endless collection of prints, her thoughts returned to the difference

Jan's presence had made to this house. The whole place felt different now that he was here. It even *sounded* different.

Analysing the new sound trickling through the house, Geraldine realised that it was coming from the garden.

She got up, and went to the window to look out. The difference was immediately obvious.

The marble fountain in the garden, which had been silent and still on her arrival here, was now gurgling joyously with life.

'I wish I'd asked for your help before I started!' Geraldine told Anna ruefully, as they were stopping work for the day. 'You really are the expert on this collection.'

'It has been my life's work,' she said simply.

'Well, you've helped me enormously this afternoon. I'm very grateful.'

'You and your colleague asked for catalogues yesterday,' the old lady said, with another almost-smile. 'We never made one because we never needed one. *I* am the catalogue of this collection, Miss Simpson.'

'I appreciate that now. And please call me Geraldine—I share your dislike of the title "Miss".' Geraldine sighed as she touched the folders with her slender fingers. 'I can't help feeling what a shame it is that this collection has to be broken up. At first I thought that your uncle must have been a random hoarder. I'm beginning to realise that he had profound artistic insight. All these works of art somehow belong together.'

Anna Breydel's silvery eyes gleamed. 'I had a dream once, Geraldine. That the collection *would* stay intact. That this house would be turned into a museum—restored and well cared-for—and that people would come from all over the world to see the treasures that Cornelius Breydel had gathered here.' The light faded from her eyes. 'But that dream crumbled into dust when Cornelius passed away, and left everything to Jan.'

Geraldine shook her head. 'Have you ever suggested the idea to Jan?'

'Once. It was no use. He has made his mind up, I'm afraid. And when Jan makes his mind up no force on earth can change him. I know he'll regret it, bitterly, later on. But what can I do?'

'But why *is* he so keen to sell it all?' Geraldine queried. 'He doesn't look as though he needs the money.'

'He doesn't. He's a very wealthy man. The factories he told you about—they are immense. He supplies some of the biggest car-makers in Europe with parts for their engines.' Anna smiled her frosty smile. 'This house and everything in it don't amount to anything significant compared to what Jan already possesses.'

'Then it almost seems as if his desire to sell up is something personal.'

'Yes. It's personal.'

'He talks as though. . .almost as though he hates this place.'

The old lady reached out and picked up one of the prints in her wrinkled fingers. 'Jan is an unusual man,' she said with a sigh. 'To understand him, you have to understand something about his life. Jan was—but why should I bore you with our family history?'

'I'm not bored in the slightest,' Geraldine said quickly. 'On the contrary, I'm fascinated. Please go on, Anna.'

'Well,' Anna said, 'Jan did not have a very happy childhood. His parents separated when he was hardly more than a baby, and neither of them wanted the responsibility of raising the little boy. They were pleasure-loving people, you see, and both very selfish. God forgive me for saying that,' she added, 'as they're both dead now. But Jan spent his whole childhood being shuffled from one distant relation to another. He was lonely and neglected, and there was not much love in his life.'

'Poor child!' Geraldine exclaimed with instinctive sympathy.

'Yes. It was very sad. Jan used to come here, to this house, every Sunday. Cornelius and I would try and amuse the boy, but unfortunately neither of us knew very much about boys. Neither of us,' she explained drily, 'had ever had much to do with children. And we were already middle-aged people. So we thought little Jan would share our interest in the collection. It didn't occur to us that a seven-year-old boy might not be as enthusiastic about paintings and etchings as we were. When I think back to the hours and hours that poor child spent in the gallery with us, poring over the canvases. . .' Anna shook her head sadly. 'We didn't know any better. We weren't trying to be cruel, of course. We tried to instil what we knew into him. Cornelius and I taught him all about art. How to tell a good painting from a bad one. How the Impressionists differed from the Old Masters. About drawing and perspective and colour. He soon developed an excellent eye. You saw that this morning.'

'Indeed, I did.'

'But how he must have loathed those dreary Sundays! How much loneliness and boredom he must have endured to please us! When I think of it now, I'm amazed at the strength of character the child showed.'

'The same strength of character that the man has,' Geraldine said quietly.

'Yes, the same strength. As soon as he became a man—and Jan matured very young—he began carving out his own life. He has created wealth, success, achievement. But I'm afraid that he will always associate this house, and the collection of paintings in the gallery, with his unhappy childhood.'

'But that's awful!'

'It's very sad for him.'

'It's worse for you,' Geraldine said. 'This is your home! Where will you live when this house is sold?'

'I'll go and live with Jan in Brussels,' the old lady replied calmly. 'That's what he has wanted for years.'

'With *Jan*?' Geraldine repeated.

The old lady caught her wide-eyed expression. 'Are you surprised?' she asked drily. 'Did you think that Jan and I were deadly enemies?'

'Well, Stuart and I certainly got the impression that the two of you weren't on the best of terms.'

'We disagree violently about what should be done with this house,' Anna nodded. 'That is certain. But what are we talking about, in the end? Bricks and mortar. A little paint that has long since dried on some squares of canvas. Jan is my flesh and blood, Geraldine. I was the only mother he had as a boy, poor substitute though I was. He loves me. And I love Jan. Despite appearances to the contrary!'

'I see,' Geraldine said slowly, thinking back to the way Jan Breydel had reacted when Stuart had asked him to keep Anna 'out of their hair'. No wonder Stu had received such a brusque answer!

'Jan is a wonderful man,' Anna said gently. 'The most wonderful man I know. He has astonishing qualities. He has carved an empire out of nothing, virtually single-handed. Out of loneliness and neglect, he has created a dazzling success. He inherited nothing from his parents, Geraldine. They had spent everything by the time they died. And Cornelius never had any cash to part with—he spent every penny on art. Jan had to do it all himself. But he hasn't become hard and cold in the process, the way so many successful men do. He has never lost his warmth, and, above all, he has never lost his sense of humour.' Anna paused. 'But somewhere deep inside him,' she continued quietly, 'will always be that lonely, neglected little boy. By selling this house, I believe that Jan hopes to exorcise that pain for ever. Cut out that part of his life.'

Geraldine was staring absently at her own hands. She had just learned a great deal about Jan Breydel, and she felt oddly saddened by what she'd learned.

'He can't be a perfect paragon,' she said. 'He must have *some* faults. You said he was a womaniser and a playboy.'

'That isn't exactly what I said,' Anna corrected her gently. 'I said he liked blondes and nightclubs. But it's true that women adore Jan. They always have adored him, since he was twelve years old. But though a great many have tried, none of them has ever managed to pin Jan down. He always seems to leave them behind him. And not all of them seem to be able to cope with the experience.'

So let that be a warning to you, Geraldine thought to herself, noting the way Anna's silvery eyes met hers.

As they packed up, she recalled what Jan had said to her about the collection when they'd first met: 'I had it rammed down my throat every Sunday. If you had any idea how I loathe this house and those mouldy old canvases. . .'

But it was a terrible shame, she couldn't help thinking, that such a superb collection of paintings should go under the hammer. It all seemed to fit so perfectly—these fine works of art in this splendid old house. Anna was right. What a marvellous art gallery this house would make! People would certainly come from far and wide to see it. If only someone could get Jan to appreciate that.

But who? If Anna, the closest thing to a mother that he'd had, could not convince him, who could?

It was a great shame.

It only occurred to her as they locked up the library that her train of thought was not exactly a suitable one for a loyal employee of Horwood & Littlejohn! It was hardly the duty of auctioneers to try and persuade potential clients *not* to sell up, but to keep their goods! If she wasn't careful, she was going to have a conflict of interests here.

Keep your nose out of this, she told herself firmly, pocketing the key of the library. It's none of your business, girl. None of your business whatsoever.

Dinner was not exactly a relaxed affair. What Anna had told Geraldine about Jan Breydel had subdued her in an odd way. She could no longer look at him in quite the same way, now that she knew something about his childhood. She was, besides, preoccupied with thoughts of the collection of prints and drawings she was expected to catalogue and value. So she did not say much.

Stuart was also in a somewhat uncommunicative mood, for reasons of his own. He was clearly enjoying this assignment a great deal less than Geraldine was. Anna was, as always, aloof and reserved. And even Jan himself, usually so full of high spirits, seemed pensive. Perhaps his afternoon on the telephone had not been successful.

'Just how depressed *is* the art market at the moment?' he asked Stuart at one point.

'It's not at its best,' Stuart admitted. 'But,' he added swiftly, 'that doesn't mean this collection won't fetch good prices at auction. It's going to arouse a lot of interest in the international art-collecting community. I think I can guarantee that some of the top Far Eastern collectors will be there—and I'm sure you know that they have both superb taste and the funds to back it up.'

Jan grunted. 'Who exactly are the buyers likely to be?'

'Most of the buyers are corporate these days,' Stuart replied.

Jan glanced at Geraldine. 'Corporate?'

'Private collectors like your great-uncle Cornelius are growing rarer and rarer,' she told him. 'No matter how rich they are, individuals just don't have the funds to keep up with spiralling prices any more, all except a very few billionaires. Even the museums are struggling to keep up. That means that art—really fine art, like the collection you own—tends to get bought by commercial institutions such as banks, insurance companies, finance houses, that sort of thing.'

'Who are only interested in investment,' Jan said drily.

'Oh, they almost always put the paintings they buy on display,' Stuart said hurriedly. 'The works of art aren't lost by any means. The public can still go and see them, which is more than was the case in this house.'

'Is that true?' Jan asked Geraldine directly, looking into her eyes with that hot blue gaze.

'Well,' she said hesitantly, 'yes. They do usually put their purchases on display.' She was reluctant to contradict anything that Stuart said, so she shut her mouth at that point.

Jan, however, had sensed her diffidence, and leaned forward. 'Where exactly do they display these works of art that they buy?'

'In banks and boardrooms,' she had to admit. 'Or on the thirty-second floor of skyscrapers in Tokyo or New York. The public can get to see them,' she added, seeing Stuart's angry glance, 'but——'

'But they have to get into the boardroom,' Jan said ironically. 'Or on to the thirty-second floor of the skyscraper.'

'Yes. That's it in a nutshell.'

'I see. Thank you for clarifying that issue, Geraldine.'

She dared not meet Stuart's eyes. But she hadn't wanted to disguise the truth from Jan.

She could hear the displeasure in Stuart's rather prim voice as he began, 'What Miss Simpson is trying to say,' and continued with a long and rather wordy discourse on what excellent care investors took of their purchases, and how the public still had access to the paintings they bought.

Geraldine sensed that Jan was bored by all this, and not really paying attention, but he heard Stuart out courteously enough. 'You needn't be concerned, Mr Horwood,' he said when Stuart had finished. 'I have fully made up my mind to sell, and it doesn't really concern me who buys the collection, or what they do with it. Just give me a figure I can work with.'

'You'll have it by tomorrow afternoon,' Stu said in satisfaction.

Jan nodded. 'You should really try to see something

of Bruges while you are here,' he said, dismissing the topic. 'As I was telling Geraldine, it's one of the most beautiful cities in Europe.'

'I know Bruges rather well, actually,' Stuart said with a hint of smugness. 'I've been here many times before.'

'But it's your fiancée's first visit,' Jan said, smiling at Geraldine in a way that made her feel a hot flush under the collar. 'She really ought not to miss this opportunity.'

'There will be other opportunities, I assure you,' Stuart said coldly. 'And Miss Simpson really doesn't have the time to do any sightseeing right now. As it is, she's going to be pushed for time. She has a particularly difficult job ahead of her.'

Jan's eyes seemed to be laughing inside, but he kept a straight face as he looked back at Geraldine. 'I promise not to distract you for one second,' he said solemnly. 'And the word of Jan Breydel is his bond.'

After dinner, Stuart detached Geraldine from Jan's ambit, and steered her to the salon, where coffee had been served. 'For God's sake be sensible,' he muttered into her ear. 'Don't lose us this sale before we even start!'

'Sorry,' she whispered back. 'It's just that when he asked me straight out——'

'You heard him. He doesn't give a damn what happens to the collection, just so long as he gets his money. Let's keep him thinking that way. Right?'

'Right.'

'Don't let that old witch Anna influence you, either. You have to think of what's best for Horwood & Littlejohn at this stage.'

'I know.'

'This sale means everything to Horwood & Littlejohn.'

'I know!'

'Then use your head,' he hissed. 'For once in your life, use your head!'

CHAPTER FOUR

GERALDINE was dreaming of a garden.

A beautiful summer garden. Hundreds of roses were blooming in the soft sunshine. They were so perfumed! She could smell the sweet scent of the blooms brushing her face. She smiled as the soft petals tickled her cheek, and opened her eyes. . .

'Welcome to the land of the living,' Jan Breydel murmured.

Her eyes widened in dazed surprise. He was sitting on her bed, brushing her face with a single long-stemmed rose.

'What—what on earth are you doing here?' she stammered, struggling to sit up. She groped for her clock. 'It's only—it's only——'

'Five-thirty a.m.,' he supplied with a smile. 'The sun is rising, the lark is on the wing, and I've brought you your breakfast, Geraldine.'

'*Breakfast*?'

He put the tray on her lap. It contained orange juice, coffee, and two croissants. 'Breakfast,' he repeated firmly. 'Eat up, and let's get outside.'

'At five o'clock in the morning?'

'It's the best time to see Bruges,' he said, pouring juice into her glass. 'Before the traffic and the people arrive. You can see the city as it was five hundred years ago. Peaceful. Unsullied. It's well worth the effort, I assure you.'

She blinked at him. He was fully dressed, wearing a beautiful cashmere jersey, and looking as splendid as always. She tried to summon her scattered wits. 'Jan, you're impossible!'

'Shhh,' he said, laying a finger on her lips. 'You'll wake the household.'

She gulped. The last thing she wanted was for

anyone, especially Stuart, to come and find Jan Breydel almost in her bed! 'You can't just come into a woman's room at dawn,' she said in a lower voice, 'and expect her to leap to your bidding——'

'You're so beautiful when you sleep,' he interrupted, reaching out to brush a lock of hair away from her eyes. 'Exquisite. Like an angel. It was all I could do to stop myself from climbing in next to you and——'

'Yes, I can imagine the rest,' Geraldine said hastily, gulping at her orange juice. 'But this is crazy!'

'Your employer refuses to give you time off to see Bruges,' he said reasonably. 'So we'll have to do it out of business hours. Try these croissants—they're absolutely freshly baked.'

'If Stuart knew you were here——'

'He'd burst a gusset,' Jan agreed equably. 'I won't tell him if you won't. My God, but he's a lucky man.'

Jan's eyes were drifting appreciatively downwards. When she checked, she found to her dismay that her nightgown was not doing much of a job of concealing what Stuart had referred to as her 'personal attributes'. She pulled the sheet up hastily, almost upsetting the tray. 'Look,' she said tightly, 'I don't mind getting up early to see the city, if that's what you've set your heart on. But I'm *not* going to sit and eat my breakfast—*or* get dressed—with you in my bedroom. So if you'll kindly get out of here, I'll meet you downstairs in ten minutes.'

'Make it five,' he grinned. 'I hate women who take ages getting ready. Enjoy your breakfast.'

Before she could take avoiding action of any kind, Jan had leaned forward, and pressed a warm and very possessive kiss on her lips. She closed her eyes involuntarily, then summoned the strength to push him away. 'Will you stop touching me? *Please*?'

'It was only a good morning kiss.'

'Out of bounds,' she said determinedly. 'In England we kiss strangers' cheeks. Never their lips.'

'So lips are out of bounds?' he queried innocently.

'Definitely.'

'Out of bounds to me, but not out of bounds to Horwood & Littlejohn?'

'I'm engaged to Stuart,' she said pointedly.

He considered her with that warm gaze. 'What other parts of your body are out of bounds?'

'To you,' she said in an even firmer tone, '*all* of me.'

'You mean I can't even kiss your cheek?'

'You can't touch, kiss or otherwise maul *any* of me,' she insisted. 'When I go back to London, you may shake my hand at the ferry port, if you wish to. But until then, every inch of me is off-limits.'

'And are you on-limits to Stuart?'

'What do you mean?' she asked, colouring.

'I mean, does he have a unique licence to do what you've just forbidden me to do? Or are you the sort of girl who prefers to wait until she's married?'

Geraldine's dark eyes flashed. 'I'll pretend I didn't hear that question,' she said, with as much stiffness as she could summon.

'Then I'll repeat it,' he announced calmly. 'Are you and Stuart sleeping together? Or are you taking Mother's advice, and saving yourself for your wedding night?'

'That's a most impertinent and ungallant question!' she said hotly. 'How dare you?'

'I was just wondering whether I should move you and Horwood into a double bedroom together,' he said guilelessly. 'Anna has some rather old-fashioned ideas of propriety, I'm afraid. But if you and your fiancé are accustomed to sleeping together, that can easily be arranged. I'll speak to the maids this morning.'

'*No*!' Geraldine exclaimed hastily. 'Stuart and I don't—that is, we aren't——' She choked. 'That won't be necessary!'

'Good.' Jan beamed. 'That's what I wanted to know.' He studied Geraldine's flaming cheeks admiringly. 'Which leads me on to the next question.'

'Which is?' she said through clenched teeth.

'Has any other man managed to get you to abandon

your principles? Or are you the complete innocent you seem to be?'

'You astound me,' she said, too flabbergasted even to be angry any more. 'I don't believe it. You've only known me a day or two, and you're asking me if I'm a——'

'Well?' he challenged. '*Are* you?'

She shook her head wearily. 'You have the nerve of the devil, Jan. I presume you won't let it rest until you get an answer?'

'I could ask Horwood,' he suggested sweetly. 'He probably knows the answer.'

'Don't,' she said in alarm. She swallowed hard. 'If you really must be a complete boor about it, then the answer is yes, I *am*, and I hope you're satisfied now!'

Oddly close to tears, she scrambled out of bed, not caring that he was getting a grandstand view of her bare legs, and hurried to the bathroom, slamming the door behind her.

There she nursed her stung pride, blinking away tears. Damn the man. *Damn* him! How dared he confront her with such intimate questions? What was it to him, anyway? What right did he have to trample on her most private feelings like this?

The door opened behind her.

'Oh, give me a break,' she sniffed wearily.

'I knew you'd be crying.' She felt strong arms slide around her waist, and draw her back against a warm male body. The feeling was deliciously comforting, even though it was he who had first inflicted the hurt! His voice was husky, close to her ear. 'Don't cry. If you imagine I think any the less of you now, then you're very wrong. I think all the more of you, Geraldine.' She shuddered as she felt him kiss her neck, once, very tenderly. Then he released her. 'Get dressed,' he said. 'I'll wait for you in the courtyard.'

She heard the door close, and he was gone.

The house was as still as the grave as she flitted down the corridors in a tartan skirt and a thick Aran jumper some ten minutes later. Nobody seemed to be stirring at this unearthly hour. She paused guiltily as she passed Stuart's bedroom door. She stood there in an agony of doubt. Should she tell him what she was doing, and who with?

Then she heard a resounding snore from within, and made up her mind. She would leave Stu to his sweet dreams. Sufficient unto the day was the evil thereof. Or something.

Jan was leaning against the red Ferrari, whistling. He smiled warmly at her as she emerged from the house. 'You look magnificent. The Scottish effect really suits you.'

'My grandmother came from Dundee,' she said. 'Where are we going?'

'On a magical mystery tour,' he said, opening the door for her.

She slid into the Ferrari's interior. The white leather upholstery smelled intoxicating, and when Jan got behind the wheel, and fired up the engine, Geraldine felt a thrill of excitement in her stomach.

'I've never been in a Ferrari before,' she confessed, as Jan swung the car out through the gates.

'How many wonderful new experiences lie ahead of you,' he smiled, 'you lucky, lucky girl.'

And of course, Jan had been right. There *was* no time to see the ancient city of Bruges, Geraldine thought, than early in the morning, before the bustle of modern life began.

As Jan drove the Ferrari through the almost deserted streets, she was able to drink in the beauty of it all. And she sat rapt. She'd always thought of Bruges as the city of lace, swans and quaint bridges; what she had not expected was the majesty of Gothic and Renaissance buildings that towered over the roof-tops, or the Baroque splendour of the public buildings, with their mighty doorways and ornate gables—nor, in the end, the greenness of it all. Bruges was a city of lush foliage. Setting off the architectural glories were apparently endless swathes of lawn and garden, with mighty trees of all sorts; oaks and elms and chestnuts, exquisite willows that trailed their green fingers in the reflecting canals, and beeches whose leaves shimmered yellow in the last blaze of autumn. Everywhere, the venerable stone-work was cloaked in green ivy or scarlet Virginia creeper.

'It's enchanting,' she breathed, and meant it literally. 'How many canals are there?'

'I have no idea,' Jan laughed. 'There's water in every corner of the city. The wealth of Bruges was founded on the river and the sea, over a thousand years ago. Bruges traded with every corner of the world. It became a commercial centre of international importance. Of course, there was a near-disaster in the fifteenth century, when the river silted up, cutting off the passage to the North Sea. The city's trade came to a standstill. If we hadn't turned to our other great love, Art, Bruges might have withered away and died. But we're an adaptable lot, and it wasn't long before Bruges became as famous as a centre of painting and the arts as it had been for commerce. Nowadays, both facets are equally important. I presume you came over from England on the Dover-Zeebrugge ferry?'

'Yes,' she nodded.

'That canal was only built this century. It took Bruges five hundred years to get back its access to the sea. But we're back in the forefront of European commerce, now. The future is very bright.'

'You talk about *us* and *we*,' Geraldine said, glancing at him, 'as though Bruges was your home. But you live in Brussels?'

'Brussels is the manufacturing heart of Belgium.' He smiled. 'It's just as magnificent a city in its own right, Geraldine. And, of course, the European Community headquarters are there. But there's something about Bruges that will always stay in my heart. It'll always be my spiritual home.'

'How odd.'

'Why do you say that?'

'Well, because you're selling Cornelius's house and

paintings, of course.' She studied his aquiline profile. 'If you love this place so much, how can you be so callous towards such a wonderful treasure?'

'This is the Grand Place,' he informed her, swinging the car right. 'It's the main square of the city. Those gabled buildings across the square were once the guildhalls. Now they're hotels, taverns and cafés, but they haven't lost any of their charm.'

'Yes, and that's your ancestor Jan Breydel on the statue over there,' she said. 'I know all that. But you haven't answered my question, Jan.'

'What question was that?' he enquired blandly.

'Come on. You've been lucky enough to inherit one of the finest houses in Bruges, which also happens to contain one of the most important art collections in Belgium. And all you can think of doing is selling it off as fast as you can. How do you reconcile *that* with saying Bruges will always be your spiritual home? Hmm?'

For once, Jan's handsome face was no longer wearing its usual affable expression. 'It's rather more complicated than you imagine,' he said shortly. 'That interesting old building over there is the Craenenburg house, where, in the fifteenth century——'

'Anna told me a little about your childhood,' Geraldine said, slipping the words in before he could say any more about the Craenenburg house, or what had happened there during the fifteenth century. 'Don't frown. She simply explained that you'd been very unhappy at times, and that you associated those memories with your great-uncle's house. But you're not a child any more. Can't you reconcile that pain at last, after all these years?'

Jan's heavy brows descended ominously. 'Geraldine——'

'Punishing the house by selling it won't do you any psychological good, you know.' She was ignoring his stormy expression at her peril, and she knew it. 'You'll just regret it for ever after. Don't you see, you're selling off a part of *yourself*, Jan. How can that ever help?'

'I've already told you once,' he said coldly, 'that questions of that sort are impertinent, Geraldine. None of it is any of your business. Why do you insist on interfering?'

'Well, you *did* invite us here to give you our professional advice,' she pointed out. 'I'm just trying to analyse your motives.'

'My motives aren't relevant.'

'I think they are. I think you might be making a bigger mistake than you imagine. And despite that oh, so sure facade of yours, I think that you have doubts inside. Big doubts.'

'Why do women always set themselves up as amateur psychologists?' he said bitterly. 'You must have colossal vanity and arrogance to imagine that you can begin to understand me, or my inner feelings, Geraldine. Well, you're not in the playground any more. I suggest you keep your schoolgirl speculations to yourself.'

It was his tone, more than his words, that cut into her like a whip. She was silent for a while, letting the sting recede. 'Well,' she said at last, 'I suppose I deserved that.'

Jan muttered a curse under his breath, and drew the Ferrari to a halt. 'Now I've hurt you,' he said, turning to her with a set face. 'The very last thing I wanted to do.'

'Oh, you were perfectly within your rights,' she said, trying to keep a cool tone, though her mouth trembled slightly. 'I was arrogant and vain, as you said.'

'No, I'm the one who needs to apologise. That was uncalled-for, and I'm sorry.' He leaned over, and kissed her—not on the lips, as he'd done earlier that morning, but on the temple. 'You happened to hit a nerve,' he said quietly, 'and I'm afraid I lashed out.'

'This whole expedition was a bad idea,' she said, glancing at her watch. It was by now past six-thirty, and traffic was starting to appear in the streets of the city. Some cafés were already rolling up their awnings and getting breakfasts ready for the early arrivals. 'I think we'd better get back, now.'

'Nobody at the house will be stirring before eight.'

'I'm rather tired,' she said with a brittle smile. 'I was awoken rather earlier than usual this morning.'

'But we've hardly begun to take in the beauties of Bruges,' he pointed out gently. 'We'll have to do this again.'

'I don't think so.'

'Are you going to sulk all morning?' he enquired, raising one eyebrow.

'I'm not sulking.'

'We still have an hour or two. And there's something we really must see before we go back. One more. Agreed?'

'If you insist,' she said without enthusiasm. She was finding Jan Breydel's company somewhat exhausting, to tell the truth. He seemed to play on her emotions with an ease that she was not accustomed to. His ability to wound her, or to make her pulses race, was alarming. She'd never come across the phenomenon before, and all her senses were shrilling a warning—*danger, danger*.

'There's another of Bruges' claims to fame,' Jan said, a little while later, as they passed through another handsome square. 'See that building over there?'

Geraldine's interest in architecture had been somewhat dimmed by the way Jan had snapped at her, but she turned obediently to look at a fine medieval building with mullioned windows and a carved doorway. 'Yes?'

'That's the Huis ter Beurse. It was owned by a thirteenth-century merchant named Van de Beurse, who set up a trading house here. Foreign dealers flocked here to check on the market, see how the prices were doing. And in time, it involved into the world's first stock exchange.'

'Really?' she asked.

'Really. And in fact, all European stock exchanges are still named after Van de Beurse. In Germany they call the stock exchange the *Börse*, in Italy, *la borsa*, in Spain it's *la bolsa*, and in France, *la bourse*.'

'Fascinating,' Geraldine drawled, though she was interested despite herself.

Jan smiled. 'Dry as dust, eh? Well, I promise what I'm about to show you next will be more to your tastes.'

And, a little while later, Geraldine was indeed sighing happily at the beautiful spot he had taken her to. She had almost forgiven him for his rudeness of earlier on.

'What a heavenly lake!' she said, as they wandered down the grassy bank to the water's edge. The trees and the lovely old bridge were reflected as if in a mirror. At the far end of the lake, a beautiful old sluice-gate spanned the water, with a gabled roof, and clumps of weeping willows that trailed lazily down. In the early morning sunlight, the dozens of white swans glowed supernaturally as they glided across the almost unmoving water.

'It's called the Minnewater,' Jan informed her, taking her arm. 'It's one of Bruges' favourite spots.'

'I can see why,' she sighed. 'Those swans are magnificent.'

'According to an old legend, they've been here for hundreds of years. The people of Bruges have to maintain them for all time. If you look closely, you'll see that their beaks are stamped with the letter B for Bruges, and the date of their birth.'

'I wish we had some bread to throw.' Geraldine gazed around her. It was a fairy-tale scene. At this hour, hardly a soul was stirring. There was no sound but for the occasional ruffling of white feathers. She leaned against Jan dreamily as they walked. 'This must be a good locality for poets.'

'And other people,' he said. 'The Minnewater has a special place in the hearts of the people of Bruges.'

They stopped to watch a pair of swans drifting across the lake, their slim white necks arched as though the birds were lost in the beauty of their own reflections.

'Thank you for bringing me here,' Geraldine said, looking up into Jan's eyes. 'And I'm sorry I stuck my long nose into your business just now. I had no right.'

He did not answer—not with words. As he took her in his arms and bent down, she had a giddy foreknowledge of what was coming. But even though those alarm-bells were by now clanging dementedly in her head, she seemed unable to avoid him. In fact, her treacherous lips had parted to meet his, and her throat arched back like a swan's as he kissed her.

His lips were so warm. They pressed on to hers, moulding to the shape of her mouth with loving intensity. It was a kiss of such sweet strength that Geraldine felt her head swim. The pressure increased gently, forcing her own lips to part, until the moist secrets of her inner mouth were open for him to plunder. His tongue touched her lips, her teeth, probed exquisitely into the intimate world of her deepest emotions.

She could no more have broken away than she could have flown to the moon. She was transfigured, totally under his spell. And even as her mind told her that she was insane, that she was doing the very thing that was most dangerous to her, her engagement to Stuart, and her own vulnerable heart, another part of her mind was telling her that no man had ever kissed her like this before.

She supposed, mesmerised, that he had kissed hundreds of other women like this. That it was his expertise that made her soul seem to melt within her, and the blood turn to liquid honey in her veins. What else could it be? There could be no real emotion for him, no real feeling in *his* heart for this dark stranger he hardly knew.

She felt his hand caress her side, lifting to cup one of her breasts. The sensation, even through her heavy Aran sweater, was intoxicating. As he moulded the soft swell of her body in his palm, she felt desire rush through her. She could not stop the low moan that rose in her throat, or the way her body pressed to his in response.

She had never felt any of this with Stuart, this pounding of the heart, this heat that was flooding her. Not with Stuart, not with any other man. She wanted to be possessed by Jan Breydel, to be swept up in the glorious power of his manhood.

And as though he sensed her unspoken cry, Jan crushed her in his arms, drawing her tight against his body, so that she felt the thrust of his hips against hers. In an unmistakable message that he wanted her every bit as badly as she wanted him!

She was gasping for breath as she finally managed to break away. She felt weak and reeling, and in a fury—not with him, but with herself.

'Is that what you brought me here for?' she said in breathless passion. 'To take advantage of me?'

'You enjoyed that as much as I did,' he retorted. There was a cobalt fire in the deep blue eyes now, and he wore a smile of triumph. 'I felt you respond, Geraldine. In the way a woman responds to a man she desires. It's glaringly obvious. So don't talk of my taking advantage of you.'

'You took advantage of my feelings,' she said, trying to control the way her legs were trembling. 'Just as you've done from the first moment I set eyes on you.'

'Do I affect your feelings that badly?' he asked gently.

'You don't need to ask that,' she said bitterly.

'Then maybe you should ask yourself what that means,' he suggested evenly.

'I know what it means! A man who's possessed as many women as you have learns all sorts of skills. You know exactly how to manipulate a woman's feelings, don't you, Jan? You like taking their hearts in your palm, and squeezing them until they bleed!'

'I didn't realise you were so melodramatic.'

'That's exactly what you do!'

'You're not being very fair,' he said, moving towards her again.

'Keep away from me, damn you!' She backed off from his advance. She was not going to let him humiliate her like that again. If he wanted to kiss her again, he was going to have to use force!

He spread his hands. 'I'm not that sort of man, Geraldine.'

'Oh, no? What sort of man makes a pass at another man's fiancée, Jan?' Her black eyes flashed at him. 'What sort of man tries to seduce a guest in his own house? What sort of man takes a delight in causing trouble between couples? Oh, don't bother to answer. I had you summed up within two minutes, Jan Breydel. And as soon as you started insulting Stuart to me, I knew what sort of person I was dealing with!'

He stared at her for a moment, then threw his head back, and laughed with genuine pleasure.

'What's so funny?' Geraldine snapped.

'You are,' he said. 'And I have to repeat, you're absolutely ravishing when you're angry. Right now I could eat you alive.'

She was about to make another retort until she suddenly realised that by arguing with him she was playing exactly the sort of game he liked most. The chase, the quarrel, the slap—it was all such a cliché. She snapped her mouth shut again. There were better ways of handling Don Juans like Jan Breydel. Angry appeals to their sense of honour had no effect whatsoever.

'It's been a charming tour of Bruges,' she said in a voice that was glassily emotionless, and very cold. 'And yes, I did enjoy the kiss by the lakeside. I'm looking forward to telling my fiancé all about it. But I do have to get down to work now. Would you be so kind as to take me back home, Mr Breydel?'

'You wouldn't dare tell Stuart Horwood about our kiss,' he mocked her.

'Oh, wouldn't I?'

'No. Because you know what sort of petty mind he has. He'd turn a kiss into an embrace, an embrace into the act of love itself.'

'You're so cruel!' she said, turning away from him.

He laid a hand gently on her shoulder. 'No. But I'm

a good judge of character. I don't have to tell you just how unsure of you Stuart really is, Geraldine. You're aware of his insecurity. That's why he's so jealous. That's why he's always watching you. Because in his heart, Stuart Horwood knows that you don't really love him——'

'Stop!'

'—that you don't love him,' he repeated emphatically, his fingers digging into her shoulder, 'and that he's the last man on earth you should marry.'

How she got back to the Ferrari after that, Geraldine never could remember. She presumed that Jan must have supported her. Her ravaged emotions were quivering inside her, and she was blind and deaf to the lovely city all around her.

Jan Breydel's words had been sadistic, vicious. They had not a shred of truth in them. But they had been perfectly pitched to make havoc of the cosy little world she had built up within herself. It all lay in ruins, and there was a wild trembling in her heart.

She had begun to curse the day she'd ever left Dover for Zeebrugge.

CHAPTER FIVE

IF STUART had been angry at her past 'indiscretions' with Jan Breydel, he was now seething. Being Stuart, he seethed silently and icily. His face was quite sallow with anger, and after the strained ordeal that was breakfast, he left without addressing a word to her, and thereafter barely said a word to her all morning.

Eventually, unable to bear her depression, Geraldine left her work in the library, and went to confront Stuart in the gallery. She found him on the telephone to one of his partners at Horwood & Littlejohn, checking on the likely values of the paintings.

'It's a big canvas, even for Monet,' he was saying. 'But it's a mature work. I've described the subject in detail, haven't I? The treatment of the trees and the reflections on the water are particularly fine. What do you think? Hmm, yes, that's just what I thought. Right, George. Speak to you again soon.'

He replaced the receiver, and made a long series of notes before looking up coldly at Geraldine.

'Anything I can do for you?'

'I know you're furious with me,' she said, twisting her hands, and looking him squarely in the eye. 'I shouldn't have gone off with Jan this morning. It was wrong. And I'm sorry.'

Stuart looked at her for a long while, his mouth compressed into a hard line. 'May I ask where exactly he took you?' he asked thinly.

'It was all very innocent,' she said, venturing a tiny smile. 'Jan just wanted to show me some of the sights of Bruges, and he didn't want to interfere with our work here. He took me on a tour of the city. We saw some stunning churches, and the Burg, and the first stock exchange. We ended up by going to a lovely little lake called the Minnewater.'

'Oh?' Stuart said, putting worlds of meaning into the monosyllable. His expression had grown even more wintry.

'Yes, it was lovely. Jan says it has a special meaning for the people of Bruges.'

'Indeed it does,' Stuart enunciated coldly. 'Minnewater means the Lake of Love. It happens to be the favourite place for Bruges lovers. It's their rendezvous. Their Lover's Lane. They all go there—to kiss and fondle each other in the grass!'

'He didn't tell me that,' Geraldine said. Her face had started to flame, and there was no use hoping Stuart wouldn't notice. His expression grew jaded.

'You really are a fool,' he said, shaking his head. 'Can't you see what that man is after?'

'I won't go a step with him again,' she said through clenched teeth.

'I'm surprised he didn't try to grope you before breakfast,' Stuart went on. 'It's just the sort of thing he would do—the Minnewater, indeed!'

'I must have been too quick for him,' she said, trying to sound easy. But if Stuart only knew what *had* happened at the Minnewater—but, thank goodness, he seemed not to suspect that he had hit on the truth, and even appeared a little mollified by her innocuous-sounding explanation and her obvious contrition. She hated lying to him, but she consoled herself that it was for the best.

'Well, we don't have a great deal more to do here, thank God. I'll give Breydel a valuation this afternoon, and if he gives us the go-ahead it'll mean another week of cataloguing and preparing the collection to go to London. Then we'll be free to shake the dust of Bruges from our feet.'

'What if my work on the prints and drawings isn't finished by then?'

'You'll just have to make sure it is,' Stuart said succinctly.

'Right,' she agreed whole-heartedly. After a quick cuddle and kiss, she felt a great deal reassured. She looked down fondly at Stuart. How handsome he was, with his silvering hair and intelligent eyes! When you compared him to a piece of beefcake like Jan Breydel, you just *knew* that Stuart was the better man. It would be mad to let a man like that cause the slightest unhappiness between her and Stu.

She was going to have to deal with Jan, she thought meaningfully. Something was going to have to be done to teach him a lesson.

At lunchtime, the staff had excelled themselves. A magnificent roast was served up, aided and abetted by roast potatoes and carrots, and accompanied by a fragrant, freshly baked loaf of Belgian bread.

After what had happened to her today, she had no right to have any sort of appetite whatsoever, but Geraldine was ravenous. She tucked into the excellent meal with relish, and even the way Jan's deep blue eyes kept drifting her way couldn't dim her enjoyment of the meal.

'Well, Horwood?' Jan said to Stuart. 'You promised me a valuation.'

'And you'll be pleased to hear that I have one right here,' Stuart said smugly. He passed a piece of paper across the table to Jan. On it were itemised figures for each of the paintings, together with the total sum that Stuart estimated the collection would fetch at auction.

Jan read it carefully. Geraldine knew that the bottom line was a figure amounting to several million pounds. But his face betrayed not a flicker of emotion as he finished. God, she thought—he really *must* be rich. Or else this collection meant absolutely nothing to him.

Jan passed the estimate over to Anna. She put on her glasses, and read it. Her face showed no expression, either. She passed it back to Jan when she'd finished. 'That seems a reasonably competent estimate,' was all she said.

Jan turned to Geraldine. 'What about the prints?'

'Well, as you know, prints are worth a lot less than paintings. But there's still a great deal of work to be done, Mr Breydel. I'm afraid I won't be in any position to give you a figure for several more days.'

'The prints and drawings will probably be sold at a separate sale, in any case,' Stuart put in. 'We don't usually auction oil-paintings and prints together. The two categories tend to have different buyers.' He looked at Jan expectantly. Jan folded the estimate and pocketed it.

'I'll think it over,' he promised, 'and give you my answer shortly.'

'Very well.'

'Darling,' Geraldine said to Stuart on a sudden inspiration, 'why don't we go out for dinner again tonight—just the two of us. Last time was lovely. *So* romantic.'

'Not a bad idea,' Stuart said, looking pleased. He turned to Jan and Anna. 'I hope that won't upset any household arrangements?'

'Not at all,' Jan said equably. 'In fact, I can recommend some good places to eat in Bruges.'

'That won't be necessary,' Geraldine said quickly. 'Stuart and I love exploring on our own. We'll just wander around together—won't we, darling?—and pop into the first tavern that takes our fancy. It's so much more fun that way.'

Jan's monumental self-possession didn't look dented by this little piece of by-play, but Geraldine fancied he was displeased none the less.

And within a few minutes of the end of the meal, she had a second inspiration about giving an unmistakable message to Jan Breydel.

She had gone to the gallery with Stuart, and was discussing some details with him, when she caught sight of Jan out of the corner of her eye. He was standing in the doorway of the gallery, about to come in.

Pretending she hadn't seen him, she reached up and put her arms around Stuart's neck.

'Darling, I'm so looking forward to tonight,' she said in a deliberately husky voice. 'This place gives me the creeps. It'll be wonderful to be just you and me—alone.'

Stuart looked surprised. Their relationship was warm, but so far it had not included demonstrations of affection as enthusiastic as this.

'Quite,' he said, and tried to disengage her arms from round his neck. 'But right at this moment——'

She was determined to drive the message well home to her unseen audience. 'I can't *wait*,' she said, even more huskily—and drew Stuart's astonished-looking mouth down onto her own!

She pressed to him ardently, determined to give a performance that was in every way equal to this morning's embrace at the Minnewater. More out of surprise than enthusiasm, Stuart allowed her to plaster his mouth with lipstick. He would be amazed, she knew, at the way she was pressing her breasts against him. It was very far from their usual style. But Jan had to get the central idea that she was Stuart Horwood's fiancée, and definitely *not* up for grabs!

It wasn't easy to maintain an impression of blazing passion with a man who was starting to try and struggle free. But she clung onto Stuart for grim life, even producing a sexy moan or two to emphasise the effect, until she heard a sound in the doorway, and broke free in fake-surprise.

She turned to the doorway. But Jan wasn't there any more. She heard his footsteps receding swiftly down the corridor.

'What on earth was that all about?' Stuart asked, getting out his handkerchief, and dabbing at his mouth.

'Just behaving in a fiancée-like fashion,' she said with a satisfied smile. 'Well, I'll be off to my labours. See you at dinnertime.'

Stuart's grey eyes followed her in mystification as she waltzed out.

But her feeling of triumph did not last very long. It soon began curdling into something less pleasant. Had she really had to put on that show for Jan's benefit? Hadn't she just lowered herself to his level?

She got down to her prints, and shook away the slight sense of shame. She had needed to do something. And she had done the best she could. Leave it at that.

As it turned out, their dinner together was extremely enjoyable, and just like old times—'old times' being the period before Jan Breydel had started looming over their lives.

She was gay and carefree, laughing at Stuart's jokes, and enjoying the sensation of freedom; and after they'd drunk their bottle of wine with dinner her head was swimming ever so slightly.

'I've been reluctant to bring this up before now,' Stuart said, covering her hand with his own, 'what with the firm doing so badly, and the market being so depressed. But perhaps it's time we started thinking about setting a date.'

'A date?' she smiled. 'What for?'

'For the wedding, my dear,' he said. 'Unless you'd rather not.'

'Of course! I can't think why you've been reluctant, Stu. It's a very important topic to me.'

'Well,' he beamed, 'when would suit you? It's autumn now, and I hate winter weddings. It's always either snowy or rainy, and everybody gets soaked waiting for the photographers. So that means either doing it really soon—before Christmas—or waiting until spring.'

'Oh, I couldn't possibly be ready before Christmas,' she said quickly.

He looked put out. 'Why not?'

'Well, there's the dress, for one thing. I haven't even started *thinking* about a design yet. And I'd have to give Mum and Dad fair warning. No, before Christmas just isn't on.'

'That means putting it off for another five months,' Stuart said sadly.

'But think how lovely it'll be to be married in the spring,' she consoled him. 'I'll be able to have apple-blossom in my bouquet!'

He sighed. 'Spring it is, then. March? April?'

'May,' she said firmly. 'The merry, merry month of May.'

'May's nearly *seven* months away! Oh, well.' Stuart got out his diary, and flipped the pages. 'Let's see. May the fifteenth is a Saturday. Any objections to that?'

'None that I can think of,' Geraldine replied.

'May the fifteenth it is, then.' Stuart clicked his pen, and wrote on the blank page. 'That's that, then.'

They looked at one another. Geraldine's eyes were shining. 'Well,' she said.

'Well,' he agreed. 'I think this calls for champagne, don't you?'

'We've already had a bottle of wine.'

'Perhaps they'll just serve us two glasses. Waiter!'

It seemed that two glasses of champagne were well within the restaurant's capabilities. They toasted each other, and laughed.

Later, on the way back home, they paused by one of the charming old bridges, and stared into the inky water. 'I've always enjoyed Bruges,' Stuart said pensively. 'But from now on, I shall always think of it with a special affection.' He turned to Geraldine. 'Why, darling, what is it? You're crying!'

'Don't worry,' she sniffed. 'They're tears of joy.'

To be still a virgin at twenty-four was, Geraldine sometimes reflected, somewhat unusual. To be sure, promiscuity was no longer in fashion, as people said it had once been. But when she looked round at her friends, the young women of her own age, she couldn't help noticing that nearly all of them seemed to be either married or living with someone by now.

Many already had families. Some had started dropping subtle hints that it was time she herself 'settled down' and conformed.

The ones who were still single tended to be the career girls, the ones who'd chosen a demanding profession; or the odd ones out, women who had some other overriding interest in life, and were thus regarded with affectionate condescension by their more marriage-minded friends.

She wasn't quite sure which category she fitted into.

Her parents' home in Ealing had been ordinary, a happy place. Her father still worked in the City, and was due to retire in a few years; her mother was a stalwart of the local charity organisations. They had been excellent parents, and, though Geraldine had now moved out into her own flat, she had kept in close touch with them. So had her two elder brothers, whom she adored. Peter and David had gone into business together, starting a small advertising agency which was now beginning to do really well. Family get-togethers were joyful occasions, full of jokes and laughter.

But as a child she'd always been a little different from the others. At school, she'd done well, and had genuinely enjoyed her studies—something that not everyone in her class could say.

Early on in life, Geraldine had developed an interest in history, narrowing that down during her teens to the history of art. She'd known she was going to find a career in some institution like a library, a gallery, or an art dealership. She'd read as much as she could about her subject, absorbed in the way something as apparently irrelevant as art could so accuratey reflect the larger trends of society: the precise detail and realism of the Victorians, the turbulent themes of the first half of the twentieth century, the technological abstractions of the present day. It all fascinated her—but it was hardly the sort of thing that most teenagers were interested in, and there were very few people she could share her discoveries with.

Not that she'd been a loner; just the opposite. Boys adored her for her growing beauty and sweet, laughing nature. As her figure started to blossom, their interest had deepened. But she'd also kept her girlfriends, too. She'd never used her power to steal anyone else's boy, that cruel game that pretty sixteen-year-olds sometimes delighted in.

So when she'd left school and had gone to college, it had been at the centre of a group of good friends.

College was where it was all supposed to happen. 'It' being meeting the right man, she supposed, and starting to make those happy plans for future wedded bliss.

For the majority, that had been the case. But somehow that hadn't happened for Geraldine. She'd worked hard, gone to lots of parties, had lots of different boyfriends, and in general thoroughly enjoyed herself. But no single boy had ever managed to affect her deeply enough to want to go beyond some steamy cuddling in the backs of cars.

She didn't think she'd been particularly virtuous. In fact, she had sometimes dreamed of a man who would sweep her off her feet. An Ardent Lover. A six-foot Adonis, all throbbing muscle and piercing eyes, who would be virile enough, and handsome enough, and intelligent enough to conquer her. Who would carry her to his crimson bed, and cover her naked body with burning kisses before. . .

Well. He hadn't come along. Not at college, anyhow. And when she'd left college, joined Horwood & Littlejohn, and had met Stuart Horwood, she hadn't immediately recognised him as the Ardent Lover of her dreams, either!

It had taken a long time to see Stuart as her future husband. She'd only truly accepted the idea, she had to confess, last night in that restaurant, when Stuart had gently insisted on setting a date for the wedding.

What she *had* come to realise was that the Ardent Lover of her dreams was just that—a dream. Love wasn't like that. Not *real* love. Real love meant responsibility, maturity, reliability. Not just a bit of lust.

So when Jan Breydel had described her as 'a complete innocent' yesterday, it hadn't been strictly accurate. The innocents, she knew, were the girls who'd rushed into bed with the first boy who made their hearts beat faster. The girls who were now stuck in dead-end marriages with husbands whom they really hadn't known when they'd jumped into the matrimonial trap.

Whereas Geraldine Simpson, calm, thoughtful Geraldine, had waited patiently until the right man had come along. And was now scheduled to marry him on a spring afternoon some six months or so ahead.

The thought made her fling off the sheets and sit up in bed.

She rumpled her hair with her fingers, pleased to see the sun streaming in through the window.

She got out of bed, this time without the assistance of Jan Breydel, his single long-stemmed rose, or his breakfast tray, and headed for the shower.

She turned the taps, trying to get the ancient plumbing to find a medium between freezing and boiling. She was devoutly hoping that Jan had got the message yesterday, and that today—and the rest of her stay in Bruges—was going to be free of amorous advances from that quarter! He was really the most impossible man. Physically magnificent, of course, and over-endowed with male charm. But, in terms of character, a delinquent. Amoral.

As she soaped herself, she thought with some amusement that Jan was actually not that far from her juvenile dream of the Ardent Lover. He was certainly virile, and he was certainly capable of making her pulses race! In fact, had Jan happened to come along during her college years, before she'd matured. . .

She shuddered at the thought. It would have been a disaster. An unmitigated catastrophe. By now, her life would have been very different.

She emerged from the shower, and towelled herself dry. How odd that Jan had mistaken her for the sort of fluff-brained idiot who would fall for his charms. Couldn't he see that she was not that sort of fool? Couldn't he see her maturity, her insight?

Apparently not. Apparently, all Jan Breydel could see was. . .

She studied herself in the mirror. Were her breasts really as perfect as Jan had said, or was that just another come-on line he used on every prospective victim? She recalled his touch yesterday by the Minnewater, and flushed.

She dropped the towel to run her eye critically over the rest of herself. She was proud of her figure, but also grateful for it; she'd never done anything especially athletic to earn those graceful, flowing lines. She was slender-limbed, with creamy skin that had never been troubled by those adolescent blemishes that had driven her friends mad. She had curves in all the right places, and no bulges in any of the wrong ones. Had she been planning a career in modelling, she might have wished for a little less bust, and a little more height; but, as it was, she had few complaints.

The face. . .well, she had been lucky with the face, too. She was never going to make the front cover of *Vogue*, but she was undeniably attractive, perhaps even beautiful. Her hair was a rich, glossy swathe that in some lights looked black, in others deep brown. Her eyes and mouth were her best features; she'd always felt that her nose was a little too long. Her mouth was as soft as velvet, and the extra-long lashes that fringed her eyes made them look even bigger and more sultry than they were.

As she applied make-up before going down to face the rest of the household, Geraldine wondered how Jan Breydel saw her. As fair game? As an intriguing challenge?

It annoyed her. It annoyed her like hell! The man's self-confidence was just too much! She hoped, rather spitefully, that she'd managed to make a good dent in it yesterday afternoon. If not, she told herself, she'd give him another dose of the same medicine today—and another dose after *that* if he still didn't take the hint.

But when she got down to breakfast five minutes later, she was slightly deflated to see that Jan's chair was empty. She greeted Anna and Stuart cheerfully enough, and sat down to bacon and eggs.

'Is the master of the house still in bed?' she enquired lightly.

'Jan has gone back to Brussels,' Anna informed her. 'He left very early this morning.'

'Had to get back to running his empire,' Stuart said drily. 'Couldn't waste any more time on this minor issue.'

'Oh,' Geraldine said, feeling oddly flat.

'He still hasn't given me his final decision,' Stuart went on. 'I presume he'll communicate with us before too long.'

'Jan is not a man to postpone his decisions,' Anna said. 'As soon as he makes his mind up, you'll hear from him.'

'I wonder whether he'll want to consult any other auction houses?' Geraldine mused.

'We'll have to wait and see.' Stuart shrugged.

'Oh, well,' Geraldine sighed, and reached out for some more bacon.

'Don't you think you've had enough food?' Stuart said meaningfully. 'After all, you have to think of that wedding-dress from now on, my love.'

'You're right.' She withdrew her hand guiltily.

'And now perhaps we can return to our original plan of lunching off sandwiches and tea,' Stuart further suggested. 'That would save both time and calories.'

'Yes, all right. Does that suit you, Anna?'

'Whatever you wish,' Anna said.

The house felt somehow cold, she thought as she drank her coffee. She sighed. The days of hot dinners and fires in all the rooms seemed to have departed with Jan Breydel. The house had died again. No doubt even the delightful little fountain in the garden had been turned off.

She checked as soon as she got to the library, peering out of the lead-paned window.

No. There it was, still trickling happily away. The flowing water caught diamond sparkles in the light. Feeling cheered, Geraldine got down to work.

As she sorted the prints into groups, carefully laying each one between sheets of tissue-paper, she was wondering why she had made those efforts to persuade

Jan to keep this collection. After all, he'd been right when he'd said that it was nothing to do with her. Indeed, she had been deliberately obstructing the design of Horwood & Littlejohn when she'd said those things.

The reasons were complicated, she sighed to herself, holding an exquisite Rembrandt etching in her hands. It would be foolish to deny that Anna Breydel had touched her heart. Geraldine had taken an instinctive liking to the old lady, and, though she had not yet fully unbent towards her, Geraldine was sure that her feelings were at least partly reciprocated. She was loath to see Anna's work of a lifetime scattered to the winds.

But it was far more than that. It was the collection itself, and that went right back to Cornelius Breydel.

What he had gathered together in this house was truly unique. Not just a collection of paintings, but a collection of great paintings. They had all been chosen by the same inspired taste. It only seemed right that they should stay together. It was a truly exceptional collection, and all the works, as it were, enhanced the qualities of the other works, and of the ensemble as a whole.

It was a crying shame that the vast art-loving public were never going to be able to appreciate it. All this love, all this culture, was just going to be auctioned off to the highest bidder, probably to wind up, as she'd warned Jan, in boardrooms and penthouse suites in far-flung capitals.

Anna's vision had been an exciting one. To turn this magnificent old mansion into a centre for the arts, to restore the canvases and modernise the structure, and to admit visitors.

It was even, she thought, turning to the next print, a fine Holbein, an excellent commercial proposition. That way, Jan would not only keep an appreciating asset—he'd be earning a fortune on the entrance tickets!

Why couldn't he see that?

She dismissed Jan Breydel's obstinate nature, and started writing in her notebook.

CHAPTER SIX

THE next two days passed uneventfully. Geraldine and Stuart worked hard at their separate assignments, only meeting to share a meal, or to chat briefly before bed.

The empty feeling in the house persisted. Jan's absence seemed to have cast a depression over everything. Stuart kept saying how much pleasanter it was without Jan here; but Geraldine sensed that he, too, had been affected by the gloom that had closed in when the master of the house had left.

Even the fine weather, after twenty-four hours, started to fade away; and by Friday morning it was drizzling determinedly. She looked out at the dripping garden, and mused that it would at least liven things up to have Jan here, with his wicked sense of humour and his gallant touches. His rose was still blooming on her bedside table. Geraldine loved flowers, and didn't have the heart to throw it away, even though it had disturbing memories for her.

Stuart grumbled about the weather as they shared a plate of sandwiches in the salon at lunchtime, toasting their feet before the blazing fire that Anna's servants had laid on.

'It's worse than England. Mist and rain, rain and mist. And I'm sure my bed's damp. My shoulder's giving me merry hell!'

'Your rheumatism?' she said sympathetically.

'It will be before long. Why doesn't the wretched man get in touch with us? It's been three days now. He can't expect us to stay here for ever, waiting on his word!'

'It *is* a matter of millions of pounds,' she reminded him. 'He needs to think it over carefully.'

'I don't see why. I very much doubt whether any

other auction house could get him better figures than that. I told him so myself. Even the old witch agreed.'

'I wish you wouldn't call her "the old witch".'

'Well, she's taken a definite dislike to me.'

'You shouldn't have said she was as mad as a hatter within ten seconds of meeting her!'

'I didn't say it. I didn't even whisper it! How was *I* to know she was Cornelius Breydel's niece? Or that she had radar hearing?'

'You assumed she was deaf and senile, with no good reason,' Geraldine smiled at him. 'Old people detest that. And they appreciate courtesy.'

'I don't need you to lecture me on courtesy,' he said darkly. 'I have the best manners of anyone I know.'

'Well, we all believe that about ourselves. It doesn't make it true. You're a snob, Stu. You were rude because you thought she was only a servant. Admit it!' On a more conciliatory note, she added, 'You've been the soul of politeness ever since. You'll soon win her over.'

'I don't want to win her over,' he retorted. 'I just want to get this job finished, and go home to my nice flat, my nice cat, and my nice——'

'Door-mat?' she suggested. 'Top hat?'

'Window garden,' Stuart said.

'We're really going to need a bigger place to live once we're married, you know,' Geraldine ruminated. After his wife's death, Stuart had sold his house in Islington, and had moved to a two-bedroomed apartment nearby. But it was very cramped, and Geraldine was rather sick of not having enough space. Stuart's reference to his window garden had reminded her of that, and of her dreams of a pretty little suburban garden somewhere, with a privet hedge and hollyhocks. 'My stuff will never fit into your flat. There won't even be room for my collection of Rolling Stones records.'

Stuart winced. 'I was rather hoping you'd leave those behind, actually. You know I'm not exactly mad about modern music. . .' He abandoned the topic as he saw her mutinous expression. 'Well, we'll give it some thought. But if we're talking about buying a house, we'd better make sure we manage to land this sale.'

'True,' she nodded. 'That would buy us a rather nice little shack.' Horwood & Littlejohn stood to make a commission of several hundred thousand out of the Breydel collection.

'How's work progressing?' he asked.

'Slowly,' she admitted. 'Some of the prints and drawings are proving tricky to identify. The old man had a good eye, but he wasn't always accurate about his attributions. This morning I found a Holbein labelled as a Dürer!'

Stuart groaned. 'Typical.'

'And more and more of them seem to keep turning up. There are more than we at first imagined. Even Anna doesn't know where some of them came from.'

And that afternoon, she made an even more dismaying discovery.

She and Anna, to be precise, made the discovery together. Geraldine had spotted a large old volume of art reproductions on the shelves, and asked Anna whether she could take a look at it. Anna had fetched the library ladder, and had got the book down.

But when she'd blown the dust off, and opened it, a handful of bits of parchment fell out.

Geraldine got on her knees to retrieve them. She was astounded to find a delightful drawing of a rabbit on the first piece she picked up, obviously a fifteenth-century work.

'Why, this looks like a Pisanello!' she exclaimed. 'And look at this study of leaves—it has to be Albrecht Dürer!' They gathered the rest of the sketches, and laid them on the table. It proved to be a small collection of treasures, all valuable Renaissance drawings. 'How on earth did they get in there?' Geraldine asked Anna.

'Cornelius got less and less methodical in his old age,' she said helplessly. 'He would buy works of art without telling me, and tuck them away in all sorts of odd places. He obviously had some reason for putting these in this book, but nobody will ever know what it was. It's a good job you asked to look at the book, Geraldine! We might never have known they were there.'

They both looked at the shelves, then at each other, with simultaneous horror.

'How many more drawings are hidden away on those shelves?' Geraldine gasped, voicing both their trains of thought.

Anna shook her head. 'God alone knows.'

And God alone knew how many books there were in the library. Over half of them were art books. Given Cornelius Breydel's magpie nature, there might be untold gems tucked away up there. It would take days to go through all those books. Weeks! A difficult job had suddenly become ten times as problematic.

'I'd better tell Stuart,' she groaned.

She was on her way down the corridor to see Stuart, when she heard the familiar rumble of the Ferrari's engine in the courtyard outside.

Her heart leaped in her breast, and she cursed it for doing so; but she was smiling with pleasure as she went to the window to look out.

The Ferrari was just pulling to a standstill. Jan got out, looking magnificent in a dark suit with a red silk tie.

But Geraldine's smile faded as he strode round to the passenger door and opened it. A second person got out of the Ferrari.

'Emerged' would have been a better word.

The willowy blonde wore dark glasses, and her pastel mink jacket was pulled up to her cheekbones; but that could not disguise her dazzling beauty. Nor could it hide the melting way she snuggled up to Jan.

They kissed. A long, lingering kiss that seemed to smoulder its way through Geraldine's wide eyes, and into her tender heart. Then Jan put a possessive arm round the blonde's waist, and led her towards the house.

* * *

Geraldine faced Jan Breydel, stone-faced.

'The problem,' she said in a voice that was struggling to stay level, 'is that we don't know how many more prints or drawings there might be.'

'You'll just have to look,' Jan said lazily.

'There are hundreds of books in the library.'

'Are you afraid of a little hard work?' he enquired, lifting one eyebrow.

'No,' she gritted. 'I'm not afraid of hard work, Mr Breydel.' She did not look at the woman who sat next to Jan in the sofa.

The blonde had been introduced to them all as Lisa Groenewald. Was she Jan's current girlfriend? A casual pick-up? There was no way of knowing. But she was even more beautiful than Geraldine had first realised in her glimpse through the window. She was in her early twenties, but was already one of Belgium's top models. She had the sort of face that set photographers alight, and the sort of body designed by nature to make clothes look fabulous.

She had been pleasant enough so far. Whether there was a mind behind the lovely façade, Geraldine had yet to discover. She didn't really give a damn, actually. With the entry of Lisa Groenewald into the house, her blood seemed to have frozen in her veins.

She had tried to ignore the woman's presence. Just as she was trying to ignore the casual way Jan's arm was thrown along the back of the sofa, his fingers absent-mindedly stroking Lisa's fine blonde hair.

It was not easy.

'But this means my job is going to take longer than we anticipated,' she went on.

'How much longer?' he asked.

'At least another fortnight.'

'Well,' he smiled, 'you don't take up much house-room.' He twined a golden ribbon of Lisa's hair through his long fingers, and rubbed it appreciatively with his thumb, admiring its sheen. 'You're perfectly welcome to stay here as long as it takes.'

She could only nod. Any suggestion that he might

allow the prints and drawings to be taken to London for appraisal had now vanished. She could hardly lug a library of thousands of books with her to Horwood & Littlejohn's sale rooms!

'You want us to handle the sale, then?' Stuart asked from the other sofa. They were all sitting around the fire, Anna included, drinking pre-dinner cocktails in a civilised way.

'Yes,' Jan said. 'I do.'

Geraldine saw the gleam of triumph in Stuart's eye. It was quickly concealed by his professional look—discreet and composed. 'That's very heartening. Very heartening indeed. I hope you'll let me reassure you that you couldn't have chosen a better place to sell your collection.'

Geraldine thought she heard Anna snort at that, but they all judiciously ignored the sound.

'I hope so, Horwood,' Jan said blandly, 'I hope so.' He and the blonde exchanged a warm, intimate smile. For an agonised moment, Geraldine thought they would kiss each other, but evidently that pleasure was to be postponed—until later.

'You won't regret it,' Stuart said unctuously. *He* had been in no way put out by the arrival of Lisa Groenewald. Just the opposite; he'd worn an air of smug pleasure all afternoon, and this news had put the cherry on the cake for him. He poured himself another drink with a sprightly air. It was obvious that he no longer considered Jan as any kind of a rival, not with such a dazzlingly beautiful creature as Lisa to distract him!

Well, Geraldine thought as she gulped down her Bloody Mary, she was paying for her little performance in the library. Paying in full coin. She could never have believed how much it would hurt to see Jan caress another woman, or see him look at her with that warm intensity in his eyes.

What the hell is this all about? she asked herself nastily. You ought to be relieved, you little idiot. Not sitting here prune-faced, wishing a beam would fall out of the ceiling and demolish Lisa Groenewald!

She drained the glass, grimacing at the aftertaste of the vodka. She only drank Bloody Marys because of the tomato juice, not the alcohol. She usually preferred the drink without any vodka at all—what her father called a Virgin Mary. But today she needed some kind of anaesthetic, if she was to get through the weekend, and she held out her glass for a refill.

'Sure you want another one?' Stuart said warningly. 'Two's usually your limit, darling.'

'Oh, come now, Horwood.' Jan rose, and took Geraldine's glass to the drinks trolley. 'Isn't this an occasion to celebrate?'

'Well, yes, I suppose it is,' Stuart agreed.

'Then let "darling" kick over the traces, and have three Bloody Marys.' Jan smiled. He poured what looked like an extremely generous measure of vodka into the glass, and topped it up with tomato juice, adding salt, pepper and Worcester sauce with an expert twist.

She took it with a nod, not meeting his eyes, and sank a third of it in one gulp.

'How long are you staying?' Anna asked him.

Jan sat back down next to the blonde model, and laid one hand casually on her slim thigh. 'All weekend, I'm pleased to say. I've spent too many working weekends lately. It's time I had a little. . .distraction.' He patted Lisa's thigh possessively as he spoke, and they exchanged another warm smile.

Why don't you make love to her here and now, right in front of us? Geraldine thought bitterly.

She closed her eyes as she tackled the vodka again. She wondered when it was going to start helping.

On Jan's suggestion that the kitchen table was too small for five—but in reality, Geraldine thought, to impress Lisa—they had supper in the dining-room. It was a grand room, with an ornate carved wooden mantelpiece, framing a roaring fire. There were no electric lights; the magnificent chandelier that hung from the panelled ceiling blazed with several dozen candles. Suits of armour stood all around, the fine old metal gleaming in the firelight. Underfoot was a huge Persian carpet in a resplendent shade of dark red. It was an unmatchable setting, and even Anna gave a sigh of pleasure.

'It's a long time since this room was used. I'll say one thing for you, Jan, you make this house come alive when you're here.'

'I hate to see resources wasted.' He smiled. 'But I'm looking forward to getting you out of this draughty old ruin, and into my house in Brussels. You'll be able to relax there, for the first time in fifty-two years!'

'I shall probably rust away with disuse. I've been the guardian of these works of art for so long.'

'You're the only work of art here that matters.' Jan touched his knuckles to Anna's withered cheek, a tender gesture that made her smile, and almost made Geraldine stop hating him for ten seconds. 'To me, the whole pile together isn't worth a hair on your head.'

And Geraldine believed him.

The meal was a succulent affair of chicken and leeks in a creamy sauce. 'This is a typical Belgian dish,' Jan told Geraldine. 'It's called *waterzooi*. I had the cooks make it in your honour.'

'It's delicious,' she said truthfully.

Lisa Groenewald turned to Geraldine with her perfect smile. 'Is this your first visit to Bruges, Geraldine?'

'Yes,' Geraldine said shortly, mentally adding, *and my last*.

'You must try and see something of the city while you're here.' Her English was as good as Jan's, lightly accented. 'It's a marvellous old place.'

'I've already had one guided tour so far,' she retorted.

'With Jan?' the other woman enquired.

'Yes.' Some devil made her add drily, 'He took me to the Minnewater.'

Lisa laughed, a sound like tinkling bells. Geraldine wondered how long it had taken her to perfect it. 'The

Minnewater! Trust Jan to take you there. Do you know what that lake is famous for?'

'Yes,' Geraldine replied thinly. 'I've heard.'

The silver bells tinkled again. 'Did he make a pass at you? That would have been quite in character, too!' Luckily for Geraldine, who nearly choked on her food at that point, Lisa did not pause for an answer, but prattled on gaily about the beauties of Bruges.

Geraldine ate in silence through the monologue. Lisa Groenewald was certainly the most beautiful woman she had ever met. Sitting opposite her, Geraldine felt totally eclipsed. All her rather smug self-appraisal a couple of days ago in the mirror had suddenly evaporated. Compared to Lisa's, her own looks weren't even significant! About the only thing to be said in her favour was that Lisa's perfect features were rather cold—while she'd always been complimented on the warmth of her own expression.

It didn't feel very warm as it sat on her face right now. 'I must make an effort to try and see those places,' she said, when Lisa finished. 'But I'm afraid I'm going to be rather busy.'

'Lisa and I are going out to a nightclub later on,' Jan said casually to Stuart. 'Would you and Geraldine like to come along?'

Stuart was not a nightclub person, and Geraldine expected him to refuse. But Stuart must have felt that on this occasion a little hob-nobbing with the clients would be appropriate. So he smiled.

'How kind. That would be very nice. We'd love to come.'

'Oh, good!' Lisa Groenewald said.

'That all right with you, darling?' Stuart asked Geraldine, rather belatedly.

Geraldine looked up expressionlessly. 'I don't mind at all if *you* go,' she said pointedly. 'But I'm rather tired. I think I'll have an early night, thanks all the same.'

Stuart didn't want to go after that, but she insisted she didn't mind at all, and Jan seemed so keen to have

Stuart along that Stuart couldn't wriggle out of it. So, after dinner, the three of them dressed and went out, leaving Geraldine in the house with Anna.

Geraldine prepared for bed in the foulest of moods. She felt bruised all over, as though she'd gone ten rounds with a heavyweight boxer. And there was the rest of the weekend to follow! Normally, she didn't mind her own company, but right now all she wanted was to curl up in bed, preferably with a hot water bottle, and lose her misery in sleep.

She brushed her hair in the mirror, cursing it for being dark and wavy, and not straight and golden. Would Jan and Lisa be sharing a bedroom? The thought made her wince. What was it to her, anyway?

The tap at her door was a welcome distraction from her self-torturings. It was Anna, with a cup in her hand.

'I thought this might help you sleep,' she said, offering the cup. It was hot chocolate. It smelled so warm and comforting that Geraldine impulsively kissed Anna's cheek in gratitude.

'This is *exactly* what I wanted,' she smiled. 'How did you guess?'

'I have eyes in my head,' Anna said in her dry way. Geraldine looked at her quickly, then looked away. Those bright eyes of Anna's were a damned sight too sharp for comfort.

'Well, it's very welcome,' she said lamely, letting Anna into the room. 'Sit down and have a chat before you go.'

They sat in the two armchairs that flanked the fire. Anna was still wearing her black dress and cardigan; Geraldine wrapped her dressing-gown around herself.

'I warned you, Geraldine,' the old lady said in what was, for her, a gentle voice. 'I told you not to flutter round him.'

'As a matter of fact, it was the other way round,' Geraldine said bitterly. 'Now I know what a butterfly feels like when some cruel boy sweeps his net at it!'

'Jan is not a boy.'

'I've gathered that.'

'And he is not cruel.'

'Oh, no?' Geraldine sent a skeptical glance at Anna. 'I think he is. Why else would he deliberately want to wound me?'

Anna smiled slightly. 'You think he brought the Groenewald girl here to wound you?'

'Oh, I'm sure he has other purposes in mind for her, too! But he deliberately set out to try and come between me and Stuart. *That* was hardly a generous action.'

'Wasn't it?' Anna said enigmatically. 'Perhaps it was intended as a kindness.'

She sipped her cocoa. 'What does *that* mean, Anna?'

'Jan is the sort of man who can't bear to see unhappiness in others. He feels compelled to help.'

'You could have fooled me,' Geraldine snorted. 'But I'm *not* unhappy, Anna.'

'Aren't you?'

'Of course not. And don't look at me with those clever grey eyes of yours! I know my own mind perfectly well.'

'So you're quite happy,' Anna said. 'I gather from Stuart Horwood that he has persuaded you to set a date for the wedding.'

'Yes. May the fifteenth next year.'

'A spring wedding.'

'That's right. I'm very excited.' Anna said nothing, and, after a few more sips of her cocoa, Geraldine burst out, 'Oh, for God's sake! Not you, too! Not *another* member of the anti-Stuart club!'

'I haven't said a thing against Mr Horwood,' Anna pointed out with perfect accuracy.

'You didn't have to. Look, I know Stuart was very rude——'

'Oh, that.' Anna waved an imperious hand. '*That* does not matter in the slightest. The elderly grow used to being treated as senile old fools. In many cases it's no doubt true. I am not so petty as to hold a minor demonstration of ill manners against your fiancé. But do tell me—who are the other members of what you call the anti-Stuart club?'

'You mean apart from your cousin?' she said acidly. 'My mother, my father, my two brothers, and several of my friends.'

'That sounds like a big club.'

'My mother's the only one who actually *says* anything,' Geraldine confessed gloomily. 'She's never been one to hold back advice. But I know the others agree with her.'

'What does she say?'

'The usual.'

'Which is?'

'Stuart is eighteen years older than me. When I'm forty-two, he'll be sixty. I must be mad to ignore such a big age-gap. That sort of thing. The same sort of thing you're about to say, no doubt.'

'No.' Anna said calmly, 'those aren't my objections at all.'

'So you *do* have objections!'

'I agree that it would be most impertinent of me to have any opinions whatsoever on your engagement,' Anna said, 'were it not for the fact that I'm old enough to be your grandmother. . .' She paused. 'And the fact that I've taken an unaccountable liking to you, Geraldine Simpson. Call it an old fool's eccentricity.'

'I don't call it eccentricity at all. I felt it too, as soon as we met.'

'I know.' Anna nodded. 'But I have no objection to Stuart Horwood's age. Unequal marriages are often more stable than those between couples of the same age. And eighteen years is not so much, after all.'

'Oh?' Geraldine said, heartened at this unexpected support.

'Indeed,' Anna said in a calm voice. 'My objection to Stuart Horwood is that he is a mean-spirited little man with no tenderness, no imagination, and *certainly* no sex-appeal, who will only drag you down to his level of mediocrity and unhappiness.'

Anna rose as though she'd made nothing more than a prediction that it might rain tomorrow. But Geraldine felt as though she'd been kicked in the stomach by a mule. She was dumb as she walked to the door with Anna. There Anna kissed her forehead lightly.

'Sleep well,' she said.

Sleep well.

When she dragged herself out of bed the next morning, Geraldine supposed she must have slept at some point during the night, but, the way her mind ached and her body twitched, it couldn't have been for very long. She seemed to have spent hours lying on thorns, tormenting herself with doubts and fears about her future.

She felt like the camel whose overloaded back was breaking under the last straw. Why should Jan Breydel have disturbed her so badly? Why should Anna's opinion have affected her so deeply? After what everyone else had said, those quietly spoken, lethal words had landed on her like a ton of bricks.

She looked ghastly in the mirror. Bruises under the eyes, pale cheeks, drooping mouth, the lot.

Damn the Breydel family! They had effectively wrecked her happiness. Why had she ever come here?

After her shower, she tried to repair the ravages of her sleepless night with bright cosmetics; but the effect was like putting make-up on a clown's sad face, and she wiped it all off wearily, and began again. When she'd done her best, she set off for breakfast.

They were all arriving at the same time. Lisa was stunning in a mauve silk tracksuit, her gleaming hair held back with a pair of silver combs. Jan's splended physique did justice to the denims and tartan shirt he wore, open at the throat to reveal a muscular chest on which unexpectedly dark hair curled crisply.

But if it was any consolation to her, Stuart looked even worse than she herself felt. His eyes were bloodshot, and she noticed his tongue was as furred as a cat's. He was evidently badly hung over this morning, and he groped for the coffee with the air of a man who was in dire need of a restorative. He gave Geraldine a crumpled smile as he sat opposite her.

'You missed quite an evening,' Jan informed her pleasantly. *He* seemed unaffected by whatever they had drunk last night. The deep indigo eyes were crystal-clear, burning into hers with their customary aggression. The deeply chiselled mouth wore a slightly mocking smile. 'I have to confess that I'd thought of your fiancé as a rather staid person until last night. But we discovered that the sober Mr Horwood has quite another side to his character. He certainly knows how to let his hair down.'

In those few apparently harmless sentences, Jan had managed to suggest that Stuart had made a complete fool of himself the night before. And indeed, Stuart gave Geraldine an extremely sheepish look.

'I had no idea Bruges had so many glamorous nightclubs,' he told her. 'They're tucked away in back alleys, and they have exciting décor and music—but oh, my goodness, the drinks are strong!'

'He held his liquor like a man,' Jan said, his grin suggesting just the opposite.

'Did I?' Stuart asked hopefully.

'Of course.' Jan slapped his shoulder, making him wince. 'You had a little difficulty navigating the stairs, but nothing to worry about.'

Lisa laughed her silver-bells laugh. 'It was so funny. Jan had to carry Stuart over his shoulder, all the way up the stairs.'

'How amusing,' Geraldine said with a glacial expression. She was not such an idiot as to be unaware that there was a concerted campaign going on to belittle Stuart in her eyes. She pushed her plate away, and rose. 'If you'll excuse me, I have work to do.'

'You haven't touched your food,' Jan called after her, but she ignored him.

Nor did it improve her battered feelings to contemplate the job that lay ahead of her this morning in the library—beginning to take out all the ancient volumes that lined the shelves, and searching through them for hidden hoards.

Anna had offered to help later on, but Geraldine knew she couldn't impose on Anna's frail strength for this somewhat gruelling task.

She made a start where it seemed logical, in one corner.

The books were extremely old and extremely dusty. She was sneezing and coughing almost at once. Grimly, she searched all the pages of each volume before turning to the next. After two hours, she was heartily sickened of her task. She'd hunted through several dozen musty tomes without any result other than a headache from sneezing, and vertigo from having been up the ladder so long. Maybe this was going to prove a wild goose chase, after all.

Then her luck changed. Opening a volume entitled *Rare Birds of Asia*, she encountered a sheaf of sketches that the old collector must have hidden away there at some time.

She bore them to the table in triumph, and sorted through them. Nothing spectacular, but a nice little haul, none the less. Feeling somewhat better pleased, she looked up—to find Jan Breydel standing there, watching her with an amused expression on his handsome face.

'I didn't hear you come in,' she gasped.

'You were too busy. Struck pay-dirt?' he enquired.

'They're seventeenth-century drawings,' she told him. 'Not masterpieces, and I doubt if we'll be able to identify the artists, but they're quite valuable.'

He came to her side to look at what she'd found. His arm brushed hers as he reached out to pick one of the drawings up. She flinched away from the contact. He didn't miss the movement.

'I'm not contagious, Geraldine.'

'No, but *I* am. I'm covered in dust.' She swatted herself, making clouds lift. 'See?'

It didn't drive him off, as she'd hoped it would. 'You should have worn a scarf.'

'I only have a silk one that my grandmother gave me. I didn't want to get it dirty.'

He didn't seem very interested in the drawing he held in his hand. His eyes were studying Geraldine with that uncomfortably piercing gaze. 'Well, congratulations on your find.'

Her pale face was set. It was an effort to be civil to the man. 'At least now I know I'm not wasting my time looking through all these books.'

'Who knows what else you'll turn up?'

'Who knows?' she echoed drily. 'Look, you don't have to pretend an interest in any of this, Mr Breydel. You're supposed to be enjoying a weekend away from your duties.'

'"Mr Breydel"? You were calling me Jan a few days ago.'

She wasn't in the mood to banter with him. 'Isn't your friend getting anxious about you? You mustn't neglect her.'

'You mean Lisa?' He smiled. 'She's lovely, isn't she?'

'Beautiful,' Geraldine said through gritted teeth.

'She has a brilliant career ahead of her.'

'I'm sure she has.'

'And she has such a delightful nature. So sweet and obliging.'

'That's the way you like your women, isn't it? Sweet and obliging.'

'I prefer that to ill-tempered and nasty,' he agreed equably. 'But your tone is unusually sharp. Can it be that you're jealous of Lisa?'

The accusation brought the blood rushing to Geraldine's cheeks. '*Jealous*? I wouldn't be in her shoes for a million pounds.'

'Why not?'

'She obviously still trusts you. She has a nasty shock in store for her.'

'That's a very harsh view,' Jan said.

'The truth is often harsh. And we all know your weakness for blondes.'

'Oh, I like brunettes, too. Sometimes even more than blondes.' His eyes caressed her. 'My, my. You certainly are dusty.' He brushed her arms gently.

'I'm going to be dustier before I finish,' she snapped, avoiding his caresses.

'What's the matter?' he said gently. 'You seem jumpy.'

'I have a lot to do,' she said, looking away from him sullenly.

'I told you last night, you're welcome to stay as long as you please. No need to rush.'

'This isn't the only sale we're handling, Mr Breydel,' she countered stiffly.

'Oh? You mean you have other collections of this magnitude to deal with?' he asked with an innocent air.

'Of course not,' she had to admit, though it stuck in her throat to do so. 'This is by the far the most significant.'

'Then take your time. By the way, I heard you discussing doing some sightseeing with Lisa last night. I enjoyed our little jaunt the other morning. We'll have to repeat that.'

'No way,' she said under her breath.

'I didn't quite catch that?'

'I said I was far too busy for sightseeing.'

'Geraldine, Geraldine.' He brushed her hair away from her brow, a familiar gesture. His touch was light. 'Do you still think I'm going to eat you?'

'I'm sure you're far too busy consuming Miss Groenewald,' she retorted. 'I wouldn't want you to get indigestion.'

'Lisa would indeed make a tasty dish,' he said, amused.

She raised a sardonic glance to his face. 'You mean you haven't sampled her yet?'

'I don't think that has anything to do with you.'

'No more than my own relationship with Stuart has anything to do with *you*. But that didn't stop you sticking your oar in.'

'And for that you still haven't forgiven me?' His fingers brushed her throat, tracing the smooth lines in a way that made her shudder involuntarily. 'I'm just trying to stop you from making a terrible mistake, Geraldine.'

Geraldine shook her head away. 'Please leave my hair alone. I don't appreciate being mauled.'

For the first time, there was a spark of anger in the deep blue eyes. 'Was I mauling you? I'm sorry.'

'It may amuse you to hear that Stuart and I have set a date for our wedding,' she told him defiantly.

'I've heard. May the fifteenth next year.'

'Ah, did your cousin tell you?'

'You won't be there at the altar on May the fifteenth,' he said quietly. 'Tear the page out of your diary.'

'I'll be there,' she vowed.

His calm was unassailable. 'You won't.'

She spoke with deliberately taunting emphasis. 'I am going to marry Stuart Horwood on May the fifteenth next year, come hell or high water.'

He mimicked her diction wickedly. '"I am going to ruin my foolish young life next year, come good advice or bad".'

'I would swear at you,' she snapped, 'if you were worth it.'

'Odd,' he mused, 'how mature and adult you are in your professional capacity—and what a silly child you are in your private life.'

'Just because I won't let you browbeat me? I *love* Stuart, Mr Breydel. I love him, and I know there will never be any other man for me!'

'And you've had so much experience of men,' he said drily, 'haven't you?'

'Oh, go and play with Lisa Groenewald,' she said, close to tears.

'Very well,' he agreed coldly. 'I will. But first——'

The way he took her in his arms allowed of no resistance. He was immensely strong, and the body that dominated hers was hard and muscular.

Geraldine tried to cry out as his mouth came down on hers, but his lips silenced her. It was a far more provocative kiss than the one at the banks of the lake. There was anger in it, even harshness; but, by a bitter paradox, the fierce passion in it ignited her feelings in a way that a more tender kiss might not have done.

She could never have believed how being kissed by a man you hated could set you alight!

All Geraldine's grief, all her frustration, had found a sudden outlet, and they rushed out in a blazing response. She felt the blood surge through her heart, boiling in her veins. Her eyes closed, and she clung to the powerful arms that held her, her lips parting to allow Jan's tongue to plunder her mouth.

The piercing sweetness of this moment! Nothing else mattered any more. Her pain, her anger, were all blazing up like leaves in an autumn bonfire. She revelled in their burning, feeling the searing heat brush her soul.

Jan's arms were so strong. She could feel the virile strength of his man's body enfolding her. He held her so close, so tight; she couldn't have struggled even if she had wanted to. And she didn't want to. She had never been kissed like this before, not even in her dreams!

Almost imperceptibly, the initial fierce hostility of his kiss changed. It lost none of its intensity; rather, it became tender and slow, and deliberately erotic. His tongue flickered, caressed, probed. She revelled in the way her breasts were crushed against him. She was aware of his hips moving against hers, could feel the strength of his thighs forcing between her own, until their bodies were pressed together in shocking intimacy.

Geraldine's body seemed to dissolve. Her head swam, the world around her fading, her soul floating in Jan's arms like a bird. This was a place she had never been before—a sensuous place, where she was all woman, and nothing else mattered except that the person who held her was all man. . .

When at last his arms relaxed around her, and he released her, she was transformed, another woman from the one who'd spat defiance at Jan a few minutes ago. Her lips clung to his as though begging them not to go. She felt his fingers touch her cheek, trailing down to her breasts. The pleasure of his touch was all too brief. Then he drew back. Her heavy lids lifted, and she looked up into his face. He was smiling.

'Now, tell me again,' he invited softly. 'Tell me you love Stuart Horwood, and that there'll never be another man in your life.'

She choked, and turned away. 'You bastard!'

He was silent for a while, watching her fight back tears of humiliation and pain. Then he turned and walked to the door. 'I'll take your advice, and go back to Lisa,' he said at the doorway. 'She may not have your charm—but at least she knows her own mind.'

Then he was gone.

CHAPTER SEVEN

THE rest of the weekend passed in a blur for Geraldine.

That was almost the literal truth; for, although in between meals and sleep she continued her job of locating and cataloguing the drawings, she was later unable to remember a single detail about her work, or even to say how she'd avoided making disastrous mistakes.

She must have been running on autopilot, as her father would have put it.

Jan's presence was a constant pain. Even when he and Lisa were out of the house, enjoying themselves somewhere, Geraldine could sense his warmth lingering in the atmosphere, almost fancied she could smell his skin, hear his voice.

She tried to avoid looking his way when they took their meals together. Meeting those indigo eyes gave her a jolt that was too painful to bear, and the very sight of him seemed to tear her inside. She tried to behave as though he were not there at all.

Not that he cared, apparently. He seemed in high good spirits, and even Stuart, after his initial antagonism, seemed to have fallen under Jan's spell. He laughed heartily with Jan, made jokes of his own, and on Sunday night, as he kissed Geraldine goodnight at her bedroom door, he told her, 'Jan's not such a bad fellow, after all. He has immense charm. And what a brain! Sharp as a scalpel. I must have just got off on the wrong foot with him, that's all.'

'You must have done,' she agreed dully.

'And that girl's a corker. Not much in the top storey maybe, but she knows all the top people in Belgium. Politicians, filmstars, captains of industry. Well, no wonder. She's an exquisite creature. She has superb eyes. Not to mention the most marvellous figure.' He licked his lips speculatively. 'I wonder if she and Jan are. . .' He broke off with a grin. 'Sorry. My thoughts were running away with me for a while, there.'

'Goodnight, Stuart,' Geraldine said in a tight voice.

'Goodnight, darling,' he said, kissing her cheek. He walked off towards his own room, whistling.

She watched Stuart go, unable to believe that he could be so completely unaware of her mood. He had not so much as asked if she felt unwell!

She closed her bedroom door, and undressed in the blackest of depressions. Stuart did not even seem to have suspected her misery. He seemed not to have noticed the fact that she'd barely said a word or smiled the whole weekend. Some fiancé! It was an added punishment that, just when Stuart should have instinctively been at his most solicitous, he seemed to have lost all his powers of observation.

About the only bright area in her overcast world was the thought that early tomorrow morning Jan and Lisa would depart for Brussels again, and she would have some measure of relief. She hoped she was going to get a little sleep tonight. The last two nights had been among the worst she'd ever had. . .

She lay in the dark, thinking about Jan. He did something to her, something that was both terrible and wonderful. Terrible because it shook her to her foundations, and made her world threaten to collapse in ruins around her. Wonderful because it filled her with a sweet excitement, made her heart beat with wild thoughts she'd never had before.

Those kisses of his. . .she'd never had such a clear demonstration of the power of sex. She knew she was inexperienced, but she wasn't a complete innocent, either. She'd been kissed before! She had thought she knew herself, had control over her emotions. It had taken Jan Breydel about five seconds to prove her wrong. She was unnerved.

The power of sex. . .could it be anything more than sex? She was aware of a voice in her heart that whispered dangerous rubbish about love. Love! To men like Jan Breydel, love was what a colourful mayfly was to a salmon fisherman—a pretty bait to disguise the sharp steel hook!

Yes, she knew that in her head. But in her heart, other dreams had taken root. Dreams of making love to Jan—not just for a night, or a week of nights, but for ever. . .

At the very thought of it, her body started to tremble.

She felt so trapped. The fact that she was engaged to Stuart Horwood was only one of her problems. Even if she'd been uncommitted, how could she have ever trusted that a man like Jan Breydel could be serious about her?

Oh, perhaps she'd been too harsh in dismissing the man as a philanderer. Just because he was devastatingly handsome didn't necessarily make him a libertine.

But he *was* a man whom female hearts found irresistible. The sort of man who could have any woman he set his heart on. Physically splendid, wealthy, forceful, amusing, gentle. . . Jan was the original man for all seasons. What could he possibly want with an obscure Englishwoman like herself? Next to women like Lisa Groenewald, the sort of women he was continually surrounded by, Geraldine Simpson was a drab nonentity. Once he'd possessed her, plundered her secrets, the game would surely lose its appeal. He would move on to the next conquest, and the next. . .until he met a woman beautiful enough and rich enough and stylish enough to be his wife.

But even after she'd been through all that, one awful question still remained. Perhaps she'd done the right thing in saying no to Jan. But could she possibly have been so foolish as to say yes to the wrong man?

She simply couldn't believe that.

Of course, the voice whispered, you didn't really say yes.

I did!

I want to marry Stuart, she told the voice fiercely. I love him, and he's the man for me!

She rolled over restlessly, trying to analyse her own feelings. Why were they so hard to appraise? She seemed to have lost the capacity to understand herself. She felt lost, bewildered. It was so easy for Jan or Anna—or her parents, for that matter—to cast doubt on the wisdom of her marrying Stuart Horwood, simply because it wasn't a conventional match. But she'd never been a conventional person. She would never have been happy marrying an ordinary man, with an ordinary mind.

And Stuart was exceptional. He had wonderful qualities, if only people could see beyond the age-gap. He was going to make her a marvellous husband. . .

Forget Jan, she told herself. Surgically remove him from your consciousness. It might hurt like hell for a while—but that's better than bleeding for ever!

She drifted slowly into a troubled sleep. Her self-analysis didn't stop, it just got less logical, and all sorts of weird ideas started creeping in. She was having a confused and violent argument with Jan Breydel, in which a Rolls-Royce, a white swan and a drawing of a giraffe somehow figured, when she became aware that someone had opened her bedroom door, and was shaking her shoulder.

'Geraldine! Geraldine, wake up.'

'Wha—who's that?' She groped for the light-switch. In the dazzle, she squinted at the intruder. It was Jan, wearing a scarlet silk dressing-gown. Was she still dreaming? 'Jan! What on earth—you haven't woken me to go touring Bruges again, have you? It's one a.m.!'

'It's Lisa,' he said, and she saw that his expression was worried. 'She's not well. Can you come and take a look at her?'

'*Me*?'

'It's a female problem. And I don't want to disturb Anna.'

Geraldine stifled a groan, and sat up. 'What's wrong with her?'

'You'd better see for yourself,' he said.

She clambered wearily out of bed. 'Shouldn't you call a doctor if she's sick?' she sighed as she pulled on her dressing-gown.

'She doesn't want a doctor. But I'll call one if you think it's appropriate. I want you to see her first.'

He took her arm, and led her through the silent house without speaking. She still felt disoriented, and resentful at being dragged out of her bed. But when he led her into Lisa's bedroom, her resentment vanished at once. Lisa was clearly in a wretched state. She was as white as the sheets she lay on, and there were dark shadows under her eyes. She looked at Geraldine in mute appeal.

Geraldine sat down beside Lisa, all her earlier spite and envy forgotten. She brushed the blonde hair gently away from the pale forehead.

'What is it, Lisa?' she murmured.

'Pains,' the other woman whispered, touching her abdomen. 'I usually get a few cramps each month, but this is awful. And it's much heavier than it's ever been before.'

'Then you should definitely see a doctor at once,' Geraldine said.

'No!' Lisa's fingers tightened around her own. 'I don't want a doctor. I hate doctors!'

Geraldine glanced up at Jan, who was watching them with folded arms and concerned eyes. He read the message in her face, and discreetly left the bedroom.

'Come on,' Geraldine said, helping Lisa on to her feet. 'Let's go to the bathroom and take a look.'

'I don't want a doctor,' Lisa repeated fretfully as Geraldine slipped an arm around her waist to assist her to the bathroom. 'I *don't*.'

'I promise we won't call one—unless it's really necessary,' Geraldine promised.

Ten minutes later, after having put the blonde model back to bed, Geraldine slipped out of the bedroom. Jan was waiting for her outside.

'Well?' he demanded.

'She's not well at all,' Geraldine said. 'It isn't normal to be in such pain—and she's losing a lot of blood.'

'You think we should call a doctor?'

'Yes,' she said without hesitation. 'She seems determined that she doesn't want one, but this could be something serious.'

Jan nodded. 'I know a good man. I'll get him. Will you stay with her?'

'Of course.'

He touched her cheek gently. 'Thank you, Geraldine.'

She smiled at him, and went back to Lisa. 'You're not going to like this,' she said, taking Lisa's clammy hands in her own, 'but Jan and I really think you need a doctor. Jan's gone to call one.'

'Oh, no!'

Geraldine tried to explain as gently as she could that it would be unwise to ignore such obviously abnormal symptoms, but Lisa responded with weak anger, then with tears. 'He'll make me go to hospital,' she sobbed. 'I don't need any of this! I have to work tomorrow! I've got a big assignment for a magazine, and I can't let everybody down!'

'You may not have to go to hospital,' Geraldine soothed. 'But even if you have to stay in bed for a day or two, surely they can postpone the filming——'

'*Postpone*?' Lisa echoed tearfully. 'They'll just get somebody else to do the assignment. That's what they do if you don't turn up.'

'But I'm sure they'll understand if you're ill,' Geraldine tried to calm her.

'They don't accept illness! You just get a reputation for unreliability!'

Geraldine stroked her hair gently. Her own work might lack excitement, she was thinking, but at least she didn't have the pressures that Lisa's career entailed. She'd just had a rather sobering insight into the high-stress world behind the glamorous image of modelling.

Jan must have galvanised the doctor, because it

seemed less than five minutes before he came bustling into the bedroom with his black bag in one hand, his glossy astrakhan coat testifying to a prosperous practice. He was around fifteen years older than Jan, a portly man with a full beard.

'You can leave her to me now, Jan,' he said.

Jan and Geraldine left him to examine the by now resigned Lisa in privacy.

'I think I owe *you* a cup of coffee this time,' Jan said, putting an arm round her shoulders and leading her downstairs to the kitchen.

'I hope she's going to be all right,' Geraldine said. 'All she seems to be able to think about is her next assignment, but she might really be ill.'

'Lisa is consumed with her work,' Jan replied, getting the cups. 'She treads the fine borderline between dedication and obsession. A lot of models are like that. It's a hard profession.'

'I've gathered that.' She hugged her gown to her breasts, remembering his apparent ability to see through her nightclothes. While she'd been in Lisa's bedroom, one of her questions had been answered. She'd been conscience-stricken for noticing such a thing while Lisa was so obviously unwell—but it had been obvious that Lisa and Jan were not sharing that bedroom. Lisa slept alone. And that had given her a warm pleasure that was even more shameful. It glowed in her now, though she tried virtuously to ignore it.

Sitting in the warm kitchen at dead of night, watching him make coffee, she had a vivid memory of the way he'd first come into her life, impatient at her slowness and complaining about the cold. It felt like an eternity ago now.

He smiled at her, as though reading her thoughts. 'Seems a long time ago, doesn't it?'

'Yes,' she nodded, 'it does.'

'I don't think I'll ever forget turning on the light, and seeing your face for the first time.'

'Was I that bad?' she laughed.

'No. Just the opposite,' he said conversationally. 'I

thought you were the most beautiful woman I'd ever seen.'

Geraldine felt the blood rush hotly into her cheeks. Her tone changed. 'You're very free with your compliments, Jan. It's just as well they don't mean anything.'

'You think I'm trying to flatter you?' he asked quietly.

'With women like Lisa Groenewald around you,' she replied, 'you can hardly expect me to believe remarks like *that*. My face and figure aren't up to those standards, and you know it.'

'You're wrong.' He studied her face with brooding eyes. 'Lisa has beautiful features. You have a beautiful face. There's a big difference, Geraldine. What makes you beautiful isn't just a lovely mouth, a charming nose, and dazzling eyes—though you certainly have all those. It's the expression you wear. All the sweetness of your character shines through. *That* makes you the most beautiful woman I've ever seen. Compared to you, Lisa Groenewald is a plastic shop-window mannequin. As for your figure. . .' His eyes complimented her warmly. 'It's magnificent. I wouldn't change a single detail.'

She was even more acutely embarrassed. 'I do not have a sweet character, Jan,' she choked. 'I can assure you of that.'

'Oh, but you do.' He came over to her, and touched the dark waves of her hair. 'And you've proved it tonight. You were so kind and gentle with Lisa. The way you behaved towards her shows just what a beautiful person you really are.'

'Hurry up and make the coffee,' she said, painfully aware of her own gaucheness.

'What a strange upbringing you Englishwomen must get,' he said softly. 'You tolerate insults with equanimity, but compliments make you squirm.'

'Actually, we're not very good at taking either,' she retorted. 'Two sugars and no milk, please.'

He laughed, and went to obey her. They sat sipping

the welcome brew, waiting for the doctor to finish with Lisa.

'How's your work going?' he asked her.

'Not bad. A lot to do, still.'

'Don't you get bored stiff?'

'My eyes get blurry sometimes,' she confessed. 'Then I go to the window, and watch the fountain for a while.' And think of you, she mentally added, but did not say the words.

'You like the fountain?'

'I love it. Anna was right. This house *does* come to life when you're here. That fountain somehow sums it up. Everything seems different when you're here. Somehow warmer, more alive. . .' Geraldine bit off her words, aware that her tongue was running away with her dangerously.

'That's the nicest compliment I've had in a long while,' he said gently.

'I didn't mean it like that. I only meant. . .'

'You don't know what you mean,' he said, smiling. 'That's your problem, my love.' He leaned forward and kissed her lightly on the mouth. They looked into each other's eyes for a moment. His deep blue gaze held hers. She felt her heart turn over inside her at the beauty of him, at his power.

Then he cupped her face in warm hands, and kissed her again, but not lightly this time. This time, there was a tenderness in the way he kissed her that made her bones melt. Her arms slid around Jan's neck, drawing him to her as their kiss deepened into passion.

'Geraldine,' he whispered, 'I want you. . .so much, darling. . .'

'Oh, Jan,' she said shakily. 'Don't do this to me!'

Jan ignored the plea. He was kissing her eyes, her temples, the satiny skin of her throat. His mouth was warm and possessive, its caress maddening her senses. She searched for his lips with her own, found it, moaned at the way his tongue invaded the warm moistness of her mouth.

Jan's hand moved under the folds of her gown, found

the ribbons that fastened the flimsy material of her nightie. He tugged them gently loose, and Geraldine felt his palm touch her naked skin. He caressed her, his fingertips trailing across her ribs, raising the goose-bumps of eroticism all over her body.

'Your skin is like silk,' he whispered. 'You're so desirable, Geraldine. So very beautiful.'

She whimpered as his caressing fingertips found the swell of her breasts, and began tracing the sensitive curves of warm skin. By the time he touched her nipples, they were erect and aching. His touch made her throat arch back in release, that soon turned to an even intenser need. She heard him whisper her name in a husky voice that thrilled her.

He cupped her full breast, holding her possessively in his palm. 'God, how I've wanted to do this,' he said hoarsely. 'From the moment I saw you, I wanted you!'

'Oh, Jan,' she said helplessly. 'You do something to me. . .'

'What do you think you do to *me*?' he demanded raggedly. His thumb brushed across her erect nipple, making her cry out in pleasure. 'Why can't I get you to see how right this is?'

'But Lisa——'

'Lisa's a good friend. But she's nothing more than that,' he vowed, kissing her lovingly on the lips. 'We've known each other for years. I could no more desire her than I could my sister—if I had one.'

'You could have fooled me,' she said, with something like a return to her shattered poise.

'That's precisely what I wanted to do—to fool you.' He had begun to stroke her again, his touch unbearably erotic on her sensitised skin. 'Do you think she was anything more than a stick to beat you with?'

'You—you *wanted* to hurt me?'

'Of course.'

'Buy why?'

'To try and get you to see sense. To try and make you understand. When I saw you kissing Stuart like that——' His eyes glittered like sword-blades for a moment. 'You put that show on for my benefit, didn't you?'

'Yes,' she confessed, lowering her eyes.

His fingers trailed across her flanks, light as butterflies' wings. 'Well, I thought I'd put a show on for your benefit. I wanted——'

They both heard the doctor's footsteps on the stair case simultaneously.

'Later,' Jan said briefly, drawing back. She pulled her gown closed over her painfully awakened body, and picked up her coffee-cup. Her hands were shaking so badly that she spilled half of it over the floor.

'Damn,' she whispered to herself unsteadily. 'What a fool I am.'

'Don't be ashamed,' he laughed. 'I'm in much the same condition.' He was so incredibly handsome as he smiled at her. 'I haven't felt like this since I was a sixteen-year-old.'

'I've never felt like this,' she said with dangerous honesty.

'No,' he agreed wryly. 'Come to think of it, neither have I.'

The doctor came into the kitchen, and put his black bag heavily on the table between them. 'She's sleeping,' he announced. 'I gave her an injection. There's no need to admit her to a hospital. Just a couple of days' bed-rest ought to be enough.'

'How is she?'

'She's all right now. I think the bleeding has stopped. But I'll be back first thing in the morning to check on her.'

'Well, you've earned your coffee, Dirk,' Jan said, rising to make it. 'So she's going to be all right?'

'I assume so,' the doctor replied.

'What's the problem, exactly?'

The doctor cleared his throat discreetly. 'Perhaps we should discuss this in private.'

'Oh! I'll get off to bed, then,' Geraldine said, rising to her feet.

'Stay,' Jan said, touching her arm. 'Geraldine's a

friend, Dirk. You can talk perfectly freely in front of her.'

'Very well,' the bearded doctor said. He gave Jan a strange glance, in which Geraldine thought she saw something other than professional courtesy. 'If that's the way you want it.'

'Well—what's wrong with Lisa?'

'There's nothing wrong with her now,' the physician replied. 'Of course, she's lost the pregnancy.'

Geraldine felt her blood run cold. Jan turned to face the doctor, the colour fading from his cheeks. 'What?'

'She's had a miscarriage,' the doctor said. 'It had run about six weeks, I'd guess. She wouldn't admit it, but I think she's induced it herself somehow. She's been a very silly girl, I'm afraid.' He raised his eyebrows at Jan's expression. 'Surely you realised?'

'No,' Jan said briefly. He looked very tense, now. 'I had no idea Lisa was pregnant.'

'She seemed to think you knew,' the other man shrugged.

'Me? Why should I know anything about this, Dirk?'

'Oh come now, Jan,' the portly doctor said. 'Let's not be coy about this.'

'I'm not being coy,' Jan said grimly. 'What are you saying?'

'That you were the father, of course. The girl made no bones about that.'

'*What*?' Jan was rigid with shock.

The doctor cleared his throat. 'I'm sorry, but you said I could talk freely.'

'Lisa said that *I* had made her pregnant?'

'Of course,' the doctor said, 'she might be lying. Is she lying?'

Jan met Geraldine's eyes. The pain in her breast was immense, and she knew it hadn't even begun to hurt yet. She waited for Jan to answer the doctor's question, feeling the slow, agonised thuds of her heart. Well? her dark eyes asked him silently. Did you father a child on the plastic shop-window mannequin? She saw his face change, saw all the light go out of his eyes. And she knew what the answer was.

'She's not lying,' he said heavily. 'I made her pregnant.'

Geraldine rose. 'I think I will go to bed now,' she heard a voice say in a strange tone, and realised it was her own. 'Goodnight.'

'Geraldine,' Jan said, moving forward. 'Please wait.'

'Don't bother,' she said in the same oddly controlled voice. 'I'm sure you have a lot on your mind right now, Mr Breydel.' Her eyes were dark pools of pain, and she saw his face tighten as he took in her hurt.

He didn't try and stop her as she walked out.

CHAPTER EIGHT

GERALDINE didn't go down to breakfast the next morning. She went straight to the library instead, very early. She was feeling unbearably fragile. She had cried for much of the night, and her eyes bore the traces. She'd had three bad nights in a row, and that had made her pain even harder to bear.

She climbed up the ladder, wishing she was dead. Between her shaking hands and her aching head, she was not in much of a state for work, but she drove herself to make a start. Anything was better than thinking about what had happened in the night.

One of the maids arrived around nine o'clock with coffee and a couple of croissants. She did not know which kind member of the household had thought of her, but she was grateful. She couldn't touch the bread, but she felt a little better after she'd drunk the coffee.

Shortly afterwards, Stuart arrived.

'Not want any breakfast?' he asked, kissing her perfunctorily on the cheek.

'No.'

'Ah, well. I see someone's sent you a tray.'

'So it wasn't you?' she asked.

'No, it wasn't me. What's the matter with you?'

'Nothing. I think I've got the flu coming on.'

'Hmm?' He checked her over. 'Yes,' he agreed. 'You look like the back of a bus this morning.'

'Thanks,' she said wearily. It no longer surprised her that Stuart couldn't tell a thing about her inner feelings.

'Well, you've missed the news. Lisa's been taken ill during the night.'

'Oh?' she said, turning back to her drawings.

'The doctor's ordered her to keep to her bed for a day or two. So she's staying on here until Wednesday or Thursday. And Jan's staying on as well, to keep an eye on her. Are you listening to me, Geraldine?'

'Yes, I'm listening to you, Stuart.'

'Well, aren't you sorry for the poor girl?'

He obviously had not the faintest notion of her own involvement in last night's events. Jan must have said nothing about it. She was grateful for that, at least. 'I'll look in on her later on,' Geraldine said expressionlessly.

'Well, you'll get a good example of how to keep on looking absolutely ravishing through an illness,' Stuart said.

'Oh?'

'I've just taken her a glass of orange juice.' He shook his head admiringly. 'You've got to hand it to her. The way she's coping, I mean. She's clearly suffering, but she still looks absolutely marvellous.'

'How clever of her,' Geraldine grated. 'What exactly is wrong with her?' she added, wondering what story was being issued for public consumption.

'Some kind of tummy bug, I gather. I didn't like to enquire too deeply. She's very pale. But she keeps on smiling so bravely. No long faces. Not like you! You really could learn a lot from that girl, you know, Geraldine. She's obviously had a lot of training. It shows. My word, it shows! She's so poised, so——'

'Stuart,' she said in quiet desperation, not sure she could bear much more of this, 'I feel very sorry for Lisa, and, as I promised, I'll look in on her as soon as I can. But, in the meantime, I've got a great deal to do.'

He gave her a dry look. 'You're not very good at taking criticism, are you, Geraldine?'

'I wasn't aware that I was being criticised,' she said thinly. 'Was I?'

'Call it some general advice. You'd do well to take a leaf or two out of Lisa Groenewald's book.'

She looked at her own slim hands. God give me strength, she thought. 'Would I?'

'Yes. You know, I can't help noticing how awkwardly you've behaved since we got here.'

Geraldine didn't look up. 'I'm sorry to hear that.'

'This is an important assignment. A *vitally* important sale. We're talking about millions of pounds, not thousands.' He laid a hand on her shoulder. 'I do realise that you've probably felt a little out of your depth here——'

'Have I?'

'Well, with your background. . .'

'My background?' she said quietly.

'Perfectly adequate as far as it goes, of course. . .but let's just say that I'm less provincial than you are. More accustomed than you are to moving in circles as rarified as this. We're at the very top, you know. The very rich, the very beautiful, the best families in the country—that sort of thing. I've mingled with these sort of people all my life. You still have a lot to learn.'

'So I've let you down, after all,' she said, even more quietly.

'Darling, your work is irreproachable. I have nothing but praise for that side of it.'

'What other side is there?'

He was silent for a while, as though beginning to realise that she might not be taking all this with equanimity. 'Well, if you don't know,' he said at last, 'then I can't tell you. But I *have* been disappointed, Geraldine. I won't hide that from you. Your gaucheness, your lack of judgement, your awkwardness. . .you've made a lot of mistakes. I can only repeat: take a good, long look at Lisa Groenewald. You can learn a great deal from her.'

He patted her head, and went out, whistling.

Geraldine closed her eyes, feeling the tears pressing hot and burning against her lids. I will *not* cry, she told herself fiercely. He isn't worth it. No man is. They're all pigs.

Provincial. How could he say that word to her? It wasn't even technically true. She'd been born within the London metropolitan district! It stung like the flick of a whip. She'd done her best. She hadn't realised she was embarrassing Stuart. She'd thought it was the other way round—that everyone in this household had been mocking Stuart behind his back, and he hadn't even noticed!

She gritted her teeth, and prepared to get back to work. Anger, she had just learned, was a good antidote to grief. It made you feel better. Just as shaky and weak, but marginally better.

She had been unconsciously dreading seeing Jan again this morning. She'd tried to prepare herself for the encounter, but when he did come into the library at mid-morning she almost cried out at the way her heart turned over inside her.

She turned away to hide her expression. He walked over to her, and touched her arm briefly. 'I'm sorry,' he said quietly.

'What are you sorry for?' she asked icily.

'For what you went through last night. For what I put you through.'

Geraldine took a deep breath, and turned to face him. He was all in black, wearing a black polo-neck sweater that clung to his magnificent torso, revealing the breadth of his chest, the lithe tautness of his waist. His expression was tense. He was evidently still affected by last night's events, but he had never looked more handsome. Her mouth was dry. 'It was just another entertaining episode for my scrap-book,' she said in a deliberately contemptuous tone. 'I have a lot to do, Jan. Would you excuse me?'

'We need to talk,' he said.

'I really don't think that there's anything you can say that would conceivably interest me.'

'Don't be a little drama queen,' he said sharply. 'It doesn't suit you.'

'And the role of humble apologist doesn't suit *you*,' she threw back at him.

'Geraldine——' He reached out to her, but she thrust him away.

'No! I've had enough!' She hurried towards the door, desperate to get away from Jan.

But he was there before her. He shut the door, and stood in front of it implacably. 'You'll hear me out,' he said grimly.

She clenched her fists, her breathing fast and uneven. She forced herself to meet his gaze. His deep blue eyes were stormy. Everything about Jan Breydel seemed to be concentrated in those eyes—the force, the arrogant self-confidence of the man. His dark eyebrows had come down heavily, evidence of formidable emotions. His mouth, which so often wore a sensual smile, was now compressed into a sombre line.

'I suppose you'll use force, if necessary,' she said unsteadily.

'Yes. If I have to.' He studied her face, assessing the pain that was there. 'You're in no state to work today,' he said quietly. 'You're exhausted. I can't bear to see you like this. Let's get away from this damned place, and out into the sun.'

'I'm not going anywhere with you,' she said shakily. 'Not ever again.'

'You are in my house,' he reminded her with quiet power. 'Be an adult, Geraldine. Come.'

She had no strength to resist him. His fingers bit into her arm as he led her out into the garden. It was a beautiful morning, the sun warming her skin though the air was crisp and fresh. Feeling like a prisoner, she let him walk her across the velvety lawn.

'I loathe that house,' he said, looking back at the beautiful old façade. 'I blame it for everything bad that's ever happened in my life. Even now, as I'm on the brink of getting rid of it, it's trying to destroy my happiness.'

'It's not the house's fault,' she replied bitterly. 'You can't blame it for *your* sins, Jan.'

'I hate it,' he repeated. 'It's so dark, so oppressive.'

He had taken her to a little wooden gate in the garden wall. He opened it, and they stepped out onto the grassy bank of the canal. The sunlight glinted golden on the calm water, illuminating the row of sixteenth-century houses on the opposite bank. There was a boat-house at the water's edge, and Jan unlocked the door.

'When I was a boy,' he told her, 'this was my one means of escape from unhappiness. . .'

She watched him as he hauled a pretty wooden rowing-boat out of the shed, and shoved it into the water.

He held out his hand to help her into the boat. 'Come,' he invited her.

'Where are you taking me?' she demanded.

'A few moments of relaxation. Nothing more.' His fingers closed round hers, drew her forward.

She stepped gingerly into the boat. He made her sit in the stern, beside the tiller, and threw a wool rug over her knees. 'This might be a bit ancient, but it'll keep the chill off.'

He unshipped the oars, and, with a few powerful strokes, rowed them into the centre of the canal. There he laid the oars to rest, and came to sit beside her, taking the tiller under his arm. 'The current will take us from here on.'

He put his free arm around her, and drew her close. She tried to hold her body rigid, but her head sagged tiredly against his shoulder—and soon she found that it was heaven to be held like this, drifting down the quiet stream.

With dreamy eyes, she watched the scenery float by. The old houses along the canal had infinite charm. With their gables and turrets and quaint windows, they were like fairy-tale dwellings. You expected that elves or pixies inhabited them, and peered from their ivy-clad façades at the passers-by.

In flower-pots, geraniums bloomed brightly; here and there, a great willow-tree trailed its fronds in the water like idle fingers, and in places other boats had been moored, or drifted, like theirs, with the stream.

Part of the enchantment was that there seemed not to be a modern building in sight. No skyscraper dominated the tiled rooftops, no tower-blocks loomed, no ugly modern architecture spoiled the perfection. The tallest structures to be seen were the spires of several Gothic churches—and their soft grey stone blended in perfectly with the mellow red brick of the houses.

Geraldine allowed the spell to dull her anger, and ease the misery in her heart. How sweet to pretend that the man in whose arms she lay truly loved her! How very sweet to accept the illusion that this could last, that she was his, and he was hers, for ever!

They drifted under a succession of old bridges which spanned the water. Some were very beautiful, exquisitely-proportioned and adorned with stone carvings. Others had a serene simplicity.

'This is what I would do when I was a boy,' Jan told her. 'I'd sneak away from Cornelius and Anna, and get out this boat. Then I'd drift with the stream, just as we're doing now, and watch Bruges pass by. I knew peace, then. And whenever I was on the canal, I used to dream of the day I would do this with the woman I loved.'

She turned her head away from him, and watched a group of snowy white swans drifting by. One fluttered its wings, sending a spray of jewels into the air. Why did swans so seldom fly? she wondered. All they had to do was spread those white wings, and they were soaring above the world, above pain. . .

Autumn was turning the leaves of the trees yellow and scarlet. The rich colours were reflected in the still water of the canal. They passed one of the old gates of the city, an impressive fortress which dominated the canal, its bulk echoed in the water.

Jan let the boat glide slowly towards the bank, until it drifted under the drooping branches of a weeping willow tree. They came to rest in the green shade, the prow of the boat nudging into the bank. When the boat had stopped moving, Jan turned to her. 'This is a good, private place to talk,' he said.

'More explanations, Jan? More insincere apologies?'

'No. I'm not here to ask for your forgiveness. I just want you to listen to me.'

'No, Jan! I can't bear any more lies, any more falsehoods——'

'I've never lied to you.'

'Everything you've said to me has been a lie; everything you do is false!'

His mouth tightened. 'Don't be a fool, Geraldine.'

'That's exactly what I'm trying to do,' she shot back at him fiercely. 'Not to be a fool any more.'

'Listen to me.' He reached out to take her arms in his hands. 'Geraldine, I am not what you think I am. A Don Juan. A man who seduces women for pleasure. I don't pretend that I've lived like a monk——'

'*That* much was made painfully evident last night,' she spat.

He winced. 'Very well. I deserved that. But Geraldine, believe me when I say I am a man of deep emotions. I am not given to flirtations or seducations. The surface may be light-hearted, but it is only a surface. Underneath, I have powerful feelings. Feelings that do not come easily, and do not go away easily. And I have never felt *anything* like the feeling I had when I met you.'

'Oh, for God's sake,' she said, turning away. 'Don't you ever give up?'

'Not where you're concerned,' he said harshly. 'If you think I'm just spinning you a line, then you're making the biggest mistake of your life! I mean what I say, Geraldine. What has happened between us cannot be ignored. Nor can it be undone. We're still almost strangers to each other. We have so much to learn about each other. And yet——' His voice softened. 'And yet, when I look in your eyes, I know there'll never be another woman for me.'

'*Stop*!' she said, covering her face.

'These are not words that I thought I would ever say, my darling, and if last night had not happened I would have waited some time before I said them to you. But now I have to say them. I want you so much. I want you more and more, with each minute that passes, each second that goes by. Your engagement to Stuart Horwood is obscene. I want you to break it off. I want you to come to Brussels with me, and——'

'And be your lover? Like Lisa?'

'Yes.'

'You bastard!' Her own voice sounded weird through the pounding in her ears. 'How can you manipulate my feelings like this? You *bastard*!'

She swung her palm at his face, as hard as she could. He caught her arm easily, and drew her to his chest.

Geraldine burst into violent sobs that were as sudden as her rage had been.

He held her close as she cried, stroking her hair gently. 'My love,' he murmured, his mouth close to hers, 'darling, darling Geraldine. I didn't want to hurt you. I'd sooner cut off my right hand.'

'You told me—she was—just a friend,' Geraldine sobbed, clinging to him. 'You said—said she was like a sister to you. And all the time—all the time she was expecting your baby!'

'One day I'll be able to explain about Lisa,' he said, kissing her moist eyelids. 'I just have to beg you to have faith in me for the meantime.'

'Faith? In you?' She stared up at him with blurred eyes. 'You must be mad. You admit you fathered her child!'

'You heard the doctor. It had run about six weeks. Talking about a *child* is rather melodramatic.'

'I'm sorry,' she said stiffly, wiping her cheeks. 'I can't make such fine distinctions. You seem to have no shame.'

'About what?'

'About the way you've treated Lisa!' she exclaimed.

'Perhaps you don't know all the details,' he suggested quietly.

'I'm perfectly willing to skip the details, thank you. I think I might be sick if I heard them. The fact remains that while you were telling me you'd never felt this way about any other woman you were having a sexual relationship with Lisa. Can you deny that?'

She saw tension tighten the muscles of his face. 'Why are you so obsessed with the past, my love? It's the future which matters. Love comes along like a thunderbolt. It alters your world in a flash. Whatever your situation is, it changes overnight. Suddenly, the things that seemed so important to you yesterday have no meaning any more.'

'Like your pregnant mistress?' she said cruelly. 'Very romantic, Jan.'

'I was talking about my work,' he said, making an obvious effort to ignore her vicious words. 'I should be in Brussels now, running my factory. Instead, I am floating down a canal in Bruges. Because I cannot bear to be away from you. Because I have to get you to see that I am serious about you.'

'So Lisa's miscarriage was not the reason you stayed? That was only a trivial detail?'

'You twist my words,' he said in frustration, his mouth growing harsh. 'And let me give you a piece of advice. Don't waste too much pity on Lisa. She can be incredibly foolish at times.'

'You mean it was her mistake, nothing to do with you?'

'I mean that she is not the swooning innocent she seems.'

'Nothing is as dull as yesterday's lover. Yes, I can see that.' She quietened her tone. 'Jan, please. There can be no trust between us any more. I admit that it was pleasant to be kissed by you—no sane woman would feel anything different. You are a very attractive man, and you know just how to use your power over women. But when you talk of trusting you, of a long-term relationship, of my breaking off with Stuart——' She shook her head with finality. 'I'm not such a fool as to fall for that line. So please don't say anything more. Just take me back to the house, and let's get on with our separate lives.'

He stared at her for a long while, the deep-set eyes

holding emotions she could only guess at. The gentle current of the canal rocked the boat like a cradle, and the willow-fronds whispered around them, sheltering them from the gaze of passers-by. He laid his warm hand over hers. 'Very well,' he said, his fingers twining through hers. 'I accept that you cannot trust me just yet. You think I'm a heartless Casanova, and you think I've shamefully mistreated Lisa Groenewald. But there is something else, something that even you, with your rigid ideas, cannot ignore for much longer. I'm talking about your engagement. You cannot marry Stuart Horwood. You would be sentencing yourself to a lifetime of unhappiness and unfulfilment.'

'How dare you——?'

'Don't tell me you love him again,' he said, silencing her with a finger laid on her lips. 'It's a lie. I've seen it in your eyes. If nothing else, this time in Bruges has taught you to see Stuart Horwood without the aura of glamour which you had so foolishly invested him with. You've seen the small, selfish, pompous little person behind the Savile Row suit. You've seen his real character. Break off the engagement. Don't waste remorse on him. Just do it. He doesn't love you, Geraldine. Let him marry another selfish, pompous little person. He'll soon find one.' Jan smiled into her dark eyes. 'And don't tell me that I'm only saying this because I'm determined to seduce you. You can't keep on fooling yourself for ever. You can never possibly know a minute's happiness—emotional or sexual—with that man.'

She took a shaky breath, and closed her eyes. 'Nobody has ever made me as unhappy as you have,' she whispered. 'You have a talent for making me bleed that no other man has ever come close to.'

'If you let me, you'd find that I have a similar talent for making you happy,' he replied.

She opened her eyes slowly, and found that he was smiling at her with an expression that made her heart miss a beat. 'Why, Jan?' she asked him sadly. 'When you could have any woman you wanted, why pick on me?'

'I told you. You're the most beautiful woman I've ever seen.' His voice grew soft. 'You don't know how I crave affection from you, Geraldine. Yet you never reach out to me. I'm always the one, reaching out to you.'

'Take me home, Jan.'

'I will. On one condition.'

'What?'

'That, just for once, you reach out to me. That you kiss me, without having to be coerced.'

She frowned. If that was what it took to get him to row her back to the house, then she had no choice. But her heart was beating faster as she leaned forward, and touched his cheek with her lips. 'There. Satisfied?'

He shook his head. 'A proper kiss, Geraldine. On the lips. Not a peck on the cheek.'

'Damn you,' she whispered. 'Damn you and your games.'

'We're perfectly private here,' he said. 'No prying eyes to observe.'

She looked at the magnificent mouth she was meant to caress with her own, and swallowed. Her heart was beating even faster now, and her palms were moist. She moved to him slowly, tilting her head slightly to touch his mouth with her own.

The contact of their flesh was electric. She shuddered as she pressed her lips to his, feeling all her suppressed craving rise up in her heart. She'd meant to pull away, but somehow her mouth lingered on his, lingered, then parted helplessly to allow their tongues to meet.

The liquid caress seemed to pour fire into her veins. As he responded, their kiss growing sweet and fierce, she clung to Jan like a drowning woman. He crushed her to his chest, his palms caressing her slender back with possessive hunger. Lost in mounting emotion, Geraldine pressed her breasts against him, her own hands roaming timidly across his neck, his shoulders, the muscular breadth of his chest.

She heard him groan with desire at her caress. It was happening again, the flood of passion between them. Was she doomed always to founder on her own treacherous sexuality? Did she have no control over her most basic passions, like a cat on heat?

His mouth roamed over her arching throat, his teeth almost cruel against her creamy skin, as though he wanted to bite the tender flesh. She whimpered aloud.

'Did I hurt you?' he asked her.

'What hurts me is knowing that this is all just a game to you. . .'

'Then play the game,' Jan whispered, his fingertips trailing across the swell of her breasts.

'I don't know the rules!' she gasped.

'I'll show you.' He kissed her with a searching sensitivity that intoxicated her, his hands caressing her with erotic skill. She was drugged as though by some spell, her body moving languorously in his embrace. Almost accidentally, her thigh brushed against his, discovering the virile potency of his arousal; and discovering, in his husky moan, her own ability to give him pleasure every bit as intense as he was giving her! The feeling of having a power of her own was so sweet. She pressed her firm flesh against him, shamelessly caressing his desire. She felt his powerful muscles tense against her, his fingers biting into her flesh with the surging response she provoked in him.

'You don't know what you're doing to me,' he said unevenly.

'The same thing you do to me,' she answered, her lips pressed against his. 'Playing the game you started. . .'

'If you let me make love to you,' he groaned, 'you'd have no more doubts, no more distrust.'

'That's why I'm not going to,' she replied. With a huge effort of will, she managed to draw back from his arms. 'You've had your kiss, Jan. Now you have to fulfil your side of the contract. Take us back to the house.'

His eyes probed hers, their colour seeming to be

darkened with the desire he felt for her. 'You're learning,' he said softly.

'Yes. I'm learning.' She tilted her head back, her mouth challenging. 'Well? Are you going to do what you promised? Or are you going to stoop to even lower tricks?'

He laughed softly. 'No. Like I told you, thoroughbreds can only be tamed with gentleness and honour. If you really want to be taken back to that prison, I'll take you. At least now I know that you don't hate me—despite last night.'

'Hate you?' she repeated. 'No. I'll never hate you, Jan. I thought I could. But I can't.'

He kissed her one last time, a lingering kiss that haunted her soul. 'Good,' he said. 'Let's go.'

As he rowed the boat back up against the stream, Geraldine lay curled up under her blanket, aware of the sweet pain of her desire still very much alive. It had tightened the skin of her breasts, melted her loins, turned her into a woman ready for love.

Only he could do this to her.

She had a sudden realisation that in one thing, at least, Jan was right. Stuart Horwood did not have the power to arouse her like this. She would never experience the peaks of passion in his arms. She might not, she thought with an even more distressing jolt, even be able to respond to Stuart as a normal woman.

The thought was infinitely depressing.

Sex isn't everything, she told herself. There's far more to a marriage than the pleasures of lovemaking. . .

To tear her mind away from the tormenting thoughts, she asked Jan, 'Do you really still think of the house as a prison? Even after all these years?'

'I have to admit that it has improved out of all recognition with your arrival in it,' he smiled at her. 'You light up all the dark corners, and chase away the melancholy old ghosts.'

'Thank you,' she said mutedly. She watched Jan's muscles flex under the black material of his sweater as he rowed. He moved like an athlete, his lithe waist swaying as the broad shoulders hauled on the oars. She would never in her life, she thought sadly, see a more beautiful man.

They got back to the house just before noon. Geraldine slipped up to her room to repair the dishevelment that Jan had no doubt inflicted on her. She didn't want to appear at lunch looking as though she'd just been made love to.

On her way up the stairs, she met Stuart coming down. His face was set in a mask of tight disapproval that she'd come to know only too well.

'Well?' he demanded peevishly. 'What's your excuse this time?'

'I don't know,' she said, pausing next to him. 'What have I done?'

'You know very well what you've done,' Stuart said with a bitter twist of his mouth, putting his hands on his hips. 'You walked out of the library without saying a thing to anyone. You left the door unlocked, your papers in disorder all over the table, you didn't even have the common courtesy to tell me you were going out.'

'Stuart, I am not a schoolgirl,' she said, her quiet tone contrasting with his raised voice. 'I don't have to leave my desk tidy, and ask teacher's permission every time I want to leave class.'

'That's an insolent response,' he snapped.

'Is it? Perhaps you should consider whether the way you spoke to *me* wasn't equally rude.' Her cheeks pink with anger, she started climbing the rest of the stairs.

'I haven't finished talking to you yet,' Stuart yapped at her back. 'Where the hell have you been all morning, Geraldine?'

She paused at the top of the stairs, and looked down at him. 'If you insist on knowing,' she replied tersely, 'Jan Breydel took me for a boat-ride on the canal.'

'What? You went out with Breydel *again*?'

'I needed a break,' she said. And left him standing there with his mouth open.

She had to pass Lisa's room on her way to her own, and as she did so, she felt a flicker of guilt at not having gone to see the girl yet today. She wasn't really in the mood, especially not after her brush with Stuart. But Lisa *had* suffered a miscarriage, and with an effort of will, she tapped on the door. She heard Lisa call her to come in, and she pushed the door open.

She had to unclench her teeth to smile at the blonde, who was sitting princess-like in her bed, piles of cushions around her, and a silk shawl over her shoulders.

'Oh!' Lisa exclaimed in pleasure. 'I'm so glad someone's come to see me. I was getting so dreadfully bored!'

'How are you feeling?' Geraldine asked her, sitting down on the armchair beside the bed.

'Pretty much OK, unless I get up. Then I feel dizzy. I'm coping.'

'Any pain?'

'Oh, no.' Lisa giggled, her eyes bright. She was perfectly made up, and looking a lot less pale and wan than last night. 'To tell the truth, the doctor's left me some lovely pills. I've taken so many that I'm floating!'

'Was that wise?'

'Well, I'm not very good at putting up with pain.' Lisa smiled. 'You can't be too careful, so I took extra. Have a chocolate?'

'No thanks. Lunch is due any minute.' A television set was showing a soap-opera at the foot of Lisa's bed. She switched off the sound, but not the picture, with the remote control. Her bed itself was laden with magazines, boxes of sweets, and lacy underwear. A cassette-player was playing cheerfully on the bedside table, in between a huge basket of hot-house fruits and an even bigger basket of hot-house flowers. Lisa's boredom threshhold, Geraldine thought uncharitably, must be lower than most people's. 'I'm very sorry about what happened to you,' she said.

'Don't be.' Lisa helped herself to a liqueur chocolate. 'It was a blessed relief. In fact,' she added, leaning forward confidentially, 'let's say it wasn't entirely accidental.' She smiled at Geraldine, and popped the chocolate into her lovely mouth.

Geraldine controlled her expression. So the doctor's guess had been right! 'That could have been very dangerous,' she said coolly. 'You took a foolish risk, Lisa. Why didn't you go to a clinic?'

'I didn't want a fuss. Somebody told me what to do, and I just did it. I didn't know the results would be so drastic.'

'What did you expect?'

'Well, at least I've got rid of the thing,' Lisa shrugged. 'Unplanned motherhood is definitely *not* on the agenda for my career right now. Pregnant women are so hideous, aren't they?'

'I think they're beautiful.'

'What, waddling around for nine months with your body all swollen like a balloon, and your boobs out to here?' Lisa shuddered. 'No, thanks. The only thing that annoys me about all this is missing that assignment. Still, better that than missing the next thirty.'

Geraldine sighed. She could never conceive of herself talking or behaving like Lisa. If she'd been pregnant with Jan Breydel's baby, she'd rather have died than face a termination.

Jan's baby. . .what would it look like? she wondered absently. It might have her dark hair and Jan's marvellous blue eyes. If it were a boy, he would probably inherit Jan's stunning physique, too, and grow to be as handsome as his father. She had a vision of a sturdy, laughing child with indigo eyes, reaching out to her——

'Hey! Wake up!' Lisa said, snapping her fingers in Geraldine's face.

Geraldine sat up with a start. 'Sorry. I was just thinking of something.'

'Something very nice to judge by the moony expression you were wearing. You looked quite blissful. A man?'

'A boy, actually,' she said, straight-faced.

'I prefer men,' Lisa said, selecting another chocolate.

'Like Jan?' Geraldine couldn't help asking.

'Hmm, *yes*.' Lisa wriggled in pleasure, whether at the liqueur chocolate currently melting in her mouth, or at the memory of Jan Breydel's lovemaking, Geraldine could not tell.

'Those things actually have a lot of alcohol in them,' she said coldly. 'They probably won't mix too well with your painkillers.'

'They mix beautifully,' Lisa assured her dreamily. 'And they don't affect me in any other way, either. I'm one of those favoured people who can eat all the chocolate they want, and not put on an ounce. Isn't that lucky? Do you know, I've never been on a diet for a single day of my life. Not once.' She preened. 'And look at my figure!'

Geraldine, who did not share Lisa's ability to gorge on chocolates without effect, smiled thinly. 'How nice for you.'

What on earth, she was wondering, did men see in Lisa Groenewald? She was certainly beautiful; but when you looked past the flawless complexion and golden hair you saw only selfishness and vapid narcissism.

Did Stuart really imagine she could learn anything from this shallow creature? He must know very little about either Lisa or herself.

And Jan—what possible attraction could Lisa have held for a man like Jan? Was Jan the sort of man who would make love to a fool, just because she had a pretty face? Surely he liked more of a challenge than *that*?

'You've known him a long time, haven't you?' she asked.

'Jan? Oh, yes. Since I was a child. He's older than me, of course. If I ever cut my finger or scratched my knee, he was always the one I ran to so he could kiss it better. He's been getting me out of one scrape or another all my life. He's always been exactly like a big brother to me.'

'Well, not exactly like a big brother,' Geraldine said drily.

'What?' Lisa frowned. 'Oh, yes. I see what you mean.'

'It *was* Jan's—wasn't it?' she asked the blonde, moved by a faint flicker of hope.

'Oh, yes,' Lisa nodded. 'I should have been more careful, but with Jan one tends to lose one's head—if you know what I mean. He's very. . .forceful.' Lisa snickered. 'I'm sure you can imagine.'

Geraldine felt sick. 'Yes. I can imagine.'

'Here, try one of these. They've got real cognac in them!'

A quarter of an hour later, Geraldine was sitting down to lunch beside Anna Breydel. Jan, she was told, would not be coming down to lunch; he had important telephone calls to make in the study. It wasn't entirely unwelcome news. It might have been very hard facing him across the table after what had happened between them that morning under the weeping willow tree.

Stuart ignored her pointedly. He was clearly in one of his sulks. So she talked easily to Anna, drawing the old lady out about her memories.

'Bruges hasn't changed much since I was a girl,' she smiled. 'A bit more traffic, more motor-boats on the canals. . .but it's still the same lovely, tranquil place. When Jan was a boy he used to call it a fairy-tale city.'

Geraldine had been struck by the same idea, and she smiled. 'It can't have been all bad for him, then.'

'Oh, no. At least Jan was never bored. He always had a formidable brain, even as a child. He could remember an extraordinary amount of information. He could marshal it, too, organise his thoughts, and come up with the right answer every time. Those qualities formed early. Perhaps Cornelius and I helped them develop a little as we taught him about Art. Later on in life, that brain-power of his had a lot to do with his success in business. He was always streets ahead of the opposition.'

'What was he like as a boy?'

'He was beautiful,' Anna sighed. 'But he was a solemn boy. He didn't have much to laugh about, of course. On the other hand, I don't think we ever saw him cry, either. He took whatever life offered with equal courage. He would row himself round the canals for whole afternoons at a time. Dreaming I suppose, though no one will ever know what about.'

His words echoed through her mind: 'I used to dream of the day I would do this with the woman I loved'.

'After lunch,' Anna volunteered, 'if you like, I can show you some photographs.'

'I'd like that very much,' she said, ignoring Stuart's glare of disapproval. 'Thank you, Anna.'

After they'd eaten, as she had promised, Anna brought some photograph albums down to the salon. Stuart, needless to say, was forgoing this pleasure, and had taken himself off to the gallery in a huff.

Geraldine leafed through the pages. The old lady had been right; Jan had been a strikingly handsome boy.

She felt her heart contract as she studied the pictures. There he was—the sturdy, beautiful child with the indigo eyes. Just like in her vision. Except that this child was not smiling. The face wore a solemn, oddly adult expression. She yearned to be able to bring a happy light back to that child's eyes, to make it laugh with delight.

But that child, she knew, was long gone. Buried deep inside the complex and powerful personality that was Jan Breydel.

Anna had been studying her face every bit as keenly as she'd been studying the photographs of Jan.

'You're seeing rather a lot of each other lately, aren't you?' she asked Geraldine with characteristic directness.

Geraldine looked up into the silvery eyes. 'Yes,' she confessed unhappily. 'We are. But I assure you, Anna, I've been trying to follow your advice, and stay away from him. It's just that there seems to be this. . .'

'Magnetism?' Anna suggested in her dry way.

'Something seems to draw us together,' she agreed. 'Or rather, something in Jan seems to make him want to see me.'

'And you don't feel it? You don't want to see *him*?'

Geraldine fought with the truth for a moment, but it spilled out nevertheless. 'I've never wanted to see anybody more,' she blurted out. 'Oh, Anna! I'm being such a fool! I think I'm obsessed with him. I can't stop thinking about him, dreaming about him. I know it's terribly wrong, but——'

'Why should it be so terribly wrong?' Anna interrupted gently.

'I'm engaged to Stuart, that's why! And even if I weren't, I don't believe Jan could ever be serious about me!'

'Jan has a great capacity for being serious, Geraldine.'

'Jan is also surrounded by very beautiful women. There's one in the house right now.' She glanced at Anna, wondering whether the old lady was aware of the real nature of Lisa's 'complaint'. But Anna only smiled faintly.

'Actually, there are two,' she said, closing the albums. 'My advice to you is not to worry too much, Geraldine. Fighting against the current can be exhausting. And sometimes, the current takes you to exactly the place you want to be.'

She patted Geraldine's cheek with a curiously affectionate gesture, and left her to get on with her work.

CHAPTER NINE

STUART's part of the assignment was drawing to an end. Her own still had at least a week to run. It was becoming obvious that Geraldine would have to stay on in Bruges alone.

She and Stuart were on wary, but not quite hostile terms. Lisa Groenewald had gone back to Brussels on the Wednesday of that week, looking very much her old, glamorous self. Jan had driven her off in the scarlet Ferrari, and Geraldine had been tortured by conflicting emotions as she'd stood at the window, watching them leave—relief that Jan's disturbing presence was going, grief at the knowledge that she would miss him dreadfully.

But, with the departure of Jan and Lisa, at least her relationship with Stuart had grown a lot less complicated. She knew in her heart that it could never go back to the happy innocence of those pre-Bruges days; that was gone for ever. Still, at least they were not at each other's throats any more. In fact, it was easiest to almost ignore one another, talking desultorily at meals, and concentrating on their work.

But she could not help wondering whether the engagement could continue once they got back to London. Stuart seemed to have seen faults in her which had disappointed him deeply. And she, for her part, had seen a side of Stuart that had filled her with equal disillusionment.

He came into the library around mid-afternoon on Friday, and sat on the table beside her, looking down at her neat piles of notes. 'Your boyfriend's coming back tonight,' he told her with a sardonic smile.

'Jan?' She tried to hide the quick flash of joy in her heart. 'He's not my boyfriend, Stu.'

'No? Well, no doubt you'll be gallivanting off with him again as soon as he snaps his fingers at you.'

'Don't be nasty. Is he—is he bringing Lisa?'

'How do I know?' Stuart shrugged. 'Does it make a difference?'

'Well, *you* took a great fancy to her,' she couldn't help replying.

'I only said I wished you'd learn to be a bit more like her,' Stuart said frostily.

'I know exactly what you said, and I don't——' She broke off, and bit down her annoyance. 'Oh, Stu,' she sighed, 'let's not quarrel.'

'*I'm* not quarrelling,' he replied pointedly. 'However, I agree this is rather undignified. How are you getting on?'

'Not bad. And you?'

'I'm going to photograph the collection this morning. I've just finished setting all the stuff up.' Stuart had brought his elaborate camera equipment with him to Belgium. 'After that, there's very little more for me to do.' He examined his nails with elaborate casualness. 'I'm thinking of going back to London on the Sunday morning ferry.'

'Are you?'

'That would get me back in time for work on Monday. Actually, I went and bought my ticket this morning,' he informed her. 'I can't stay away indefinitely. I have to get back to Horwood & Littlejohn. You'll have to stay on alone, I'm afraid. How long do you think you will need to finish here?'

'Probably until next weekend. Perhaps a few days more.'

He grunted. 'When we get back to London, we'll need to do a bit of talking. And I don't mean about work. I mean about us.'

Her heart sank. 'Yes,' she said dully, 'we do need to talk. This hasn't been a very happy trip, has it? I was so excited the day we arrived in Bruges. Now I feel that things haven't gone right since the day we walked through the door of this house.'

'I wouldn't say that. We managed to land the sale, after all. That is by far the most meaningful thing. Our personal problems, naturally, have been unpleasant. But they are far less important.'

Geraldine sighed again. 'I suppose you're right.'

'It was a mistake to set a date for the wedding,' Stuart went on, toying with his pen.

'In what way?'

'We rushed things. That's always fatal. Setting a date seemed the right thing to do at the time. But since then, it's come between us. It's like having a pistol pointed at your head.'

'Is that the way you feel about it?' she asked him quietly.

He glanced at her quickly. 'I didn't say *I* felt like that. I was just making a comment. I wouldn't let you down, Geraldine.'

'It's not a question of "letting me down",' she exclaimed. 'If you're having doubts, Stuart, then for heaven's sake say so.'

An odd expression crossed his face. 'I wouldn't want to lay myself open to any accusations.'

'What sort of accusations?'

'That I led you on. Made promises I didn't keep. People have ended up in court over that sort of thing.'

Understanding dawned. 'Are you talking about a breach-of-promise suit? You think I'll take you to court if you don't marry me?'

'It's been known.'

'We're not living in the nineteenth century, for God's sake!'

'Oh, it does still happen these days,' he said, his eyes cunning.

Geraldine was speechless for a moment. She did not know whether she was enraged or hysterically amused. 'Stuart,' she said at last, shaking her head, 'I don't think you know anything about me at all. You've accused me of being gauche and provincial, when I've behaved perfectly properly. You want me to be more like Lisa Groenewald—a selfish, shallow, vain woman, who is more concerned with her appearance than anything else in life. And now you think I'd take you to court if you broke off the engagement!' She was, she had just decided, angered rather than amused. 'Do you really think I have so little pride as all that?'

'The position is unusual,' he sniffed. 'I'm much older than you are. And our social positions are hardly comparable. I am not exactly a poor man, Geraldine. I *do* happen to be a senior partner of Horwood & Littlejohn.'

'And *I* happen to be a junior employee. Yes, I know that. The fact that I'm a human being doesn't count for much, I suppose?'

He looked disconcerted at her tone. 'No need to be unpleasant. But Horwood & Littlejohn have an unsullied reputation. I am exceedingly displeased that it should be in any way compromised by the behaviour of an employee.'

'Have I been that bad?'

'As for Lisa Groenewald, I'm sorry you've taken such an unreasonable dislike to her. But I can't say I'm surprised. The reason is obvious.'

'Is it?'

'She's Jan Breydel's girlfriend. And you have taken rather a fancy to the handsome Mr Breydel.' His expression was an ugly sneer. 'Did you think you'd managed to hide your little crush, Geraldine? You say you're not provincial. Well, there is nothing more provincial than a girl who imagines that a man who is vastly her social superior could take the slightest interest in her!'

She felt the blood rush to her face. She clenched her fists. 'That was a nice thing to say, Stuart,' she told him with bitter irony.

'I'm sorry,' he said at last. 'You're right. That was uncalled-for. We're both on edge.'

'I'm sorry for being rude, too.' She looked down at the drawing that lay before her. 'Do you want to break off the engagement?' she asked him flatly. 'Is that what you're saying?'

He did not reply. Slowly, she pulled the little diamond ring off her third finger, and laid it on the table. She felt very strange, light-headed and dizzy, almost as if she was about to faint. If she'd been standing up, she might have done so. As it was, she swayed slightly as she looked up at him. 'There's your ring, Stu.'

He stared at it, frowning slightly, as though at some irritating problem. 'To tell the truth,' he said heavily, 'I haven't yet made up my mind properly.'

'I see.'

'I feel I owe it to you to give you another chance. A *final* chance,' he emphasised, 'to show yourself worthy of being my wife. Are you prepared to continue the engagement on that trial basis?'

'I don't know.' She was feeling dizzier and dizzier. 'Either we're planning to get married, or we're not. How can there be anything in between?'

He hesitated, then picked up the ring, and held it out to her. 'Just make more of an effort, Geraldine. Try a little harder. For my sake. Try to behave with a little more dignity, a little more poise. It might help to imagine that we are already married. Think of yourself as Mrs Stuart Horwood. That will help. When you're faced with a choice, ask yourself, "What would Mrs Stuart Horwood do in this situation?" That ought to help order your thoughts!'

'I suppose it ought to,' she said faintly.

'And if I see that you're making a genuine effort, then I promise I'll reconsider my misgivings. Agreed?'

She took the ring in numb fingers. But she couldn't bear to put it back on. 'I'll keep this safe,' she said, putting it into her pocket, 'but I don't think I should wear it any more.'

'An excellent idea,' he said in satisfaction. 'That shows tact, Geraldine.'

Tact, but not courage, she thought sickly. She'd thought it had finally come to a head. Instead, nothing had been settled, nothing decided. 'I'm glad we've talked this through,' Stuart was saying. 'Most satisfactory. Now, can you come and give me a hand with the photography?'

Jan had not arrived by suppertime. The three of them ate in the kitchen, and then Geraldine went up to get an early night's sleep. She had worked hard this week, and she was a little tired.

Geraldine had just finished showering, and was getting ready for bed, when she heard the knock at her bedroom door. She knew who it was without having to be told. But her heart still jolted with an electric shock as she opened the door and met Jan's eyes. He was wearing a dark silk suit with a blue tie, and he looked wonderful. He swept her unceremoniously into his strong arms, and crushed her to him.

'God, I've missed you,' he said huskily. He buried his face in her hair, inhaling her scent deep into his lungs. 'You smell absolutely marvellous. Like a rose. Have you missed me?'

'Things have been a lot quieter without you,' she said breathlessly. But she knew that her own brilliant eyes and flushed cheeks were giving the game away fatally. 'Put me down, Jan!'

He kissed her with fierce possession on the lips, making her even more breathless, and released her. He shut the door behind him, and reached into his pocket. 'I've bought you a present. I couldn't wait till morning to give it to you.'

'A present?' she asked, clutching her nightie to her throat defensively.

'Here.' He laid the long, flat velvet box on her palm. It looked alarmingly expensive, and she stared at it blankly. 'What's this in aid of?'

'Our anniversary,' he grinned. 'Nearly two weeks to the day since we first met. Open it.'

She prised the lid open. Lying on the satin was a thick gold rope necklace, the intricate strands woven together in exquisite complexity. She felt as though she'd been hit under the heart by a punch.

'Jan,' she said in a queer voice, 'this is not the sort

of present you buy a woman after you've known her two weeks.'

'Maybe not. But it's the sort of present you buy a woman you intend to know a lot longer. It's by one of Brussels' foremost jewellery designers. His latest work. Do you like it?'

'It's the loveliest thing I've ever seen. But I can't accept it.'

'You don't have any choice,' he smiled. He took it out of the box, and looped it around her slender throat. She stared dazedly into his eyes as he fastened it at the nape of her neck. It felt heavy, slinky and cool on her warm skin. 'There,' he said in satisfaction. 'It suits you to perfection. I knew it would.'

'Jan, I *can't*!'

'Take a look.' He led her to the mirror, and turned her to face her own reflection. The chain did indeed look magnificent on her. It was like a fat gold snake, lovingly coiled at her throat. Jan looked over her shoulder into the eyes of her reflection. 'Look at yourself,' he said softly, 'and see the face of a woman in love.'

Was that what a woman in love looked like? With those blurred eyes, and that trembling smile on her lips? With that wonderful look of enchantment?

His arms slipped around her waist, drawing her back against him. He smiled into the mirror. 'Don't we make a handsome couple?' he murmured. 'You can't say we don't fit well together.'

And she couldn't. His rugged masculinity contrasted stunningly with her own delicately feminine beauty. Her pale, creamy skin was the perfect foil to his dark tan, her dark eyes to his indigo jewels. Jan kissed her neck gently, his lips warm and loving. She felt herself melting inside, her pulses trembling as though her poor heart were an over-wound clock.

His hands moved caressingly across her body. She watched them dreamily in the reflection as they spanned her slim waist, then slid slowly upward until they cupped her breasts. She shuddered as he caressed the soft curves, his palms brushing the aroused peaks of her nipples. Her eyes closed, her neck arched back, her head coming to rest on his shoulder. She could smell his skin, his hair, an intoxicating male smell that she loved.

Suddenly, he exclaimed softly, and lifted her left hand. 'What's this?' he demanded.

She opened her drugged lids, and looked at her bare wedding finger. Trust Jan to notice that little detail within five minutes!

'This afternoon Stuart and I had a little—discussion,' she told him.

His eyes blazed in triumph. 'You've broken off the engagement?'

'No. . .not exactly.'

'What the hell does that mean?'

'Stuart has been having some second thoughts about our marriage.'

Jan snorted. 'Has he, indeed. And you? Aren't you having second thoughts, Geraldine?'

She looked down. 'I'm being given a period of grace. If I come up to his expectations, then the wedding will go ahead.'

'Come up to *his* expectations?' he echoed contemptuously.

'He feels I've behaved badly lately. Sullied the reputation of Horwood & Littlejohn.'

'How?'

'He thinks I don't have any manners. That my background lets me down.'

'You have immaculate manners. And your upbringing has obviously been flawless. In fact, I can't wait to meet your family.'

Geraldine laughed. 'You always make me feel better.'

Jan was not smiling. 'I mean every word I say. I've never met a woman who had your delicacy, your grace. If Horwood said those unforgivable things,' Jan said forcefully, 'then the engagement is surely off?'

'I told you. He's giving me a trial period.'

'Damn his insolence,' Jan said in a bleak voice. 'And damn your soft woman's heart! Why didn't you break it off while you had the chance?'

'It wasn't like that,' she said miserably.

'So you're still supposedly engaged to Stuart Horwood?'

'Yes, I suppose so. . .'

'But you aren't wearing his ring any more!'

'No.' She glanced at the dressing-table, where Stuart's engagement ring lay in a saucer. 'But I'm still his fiancée.'

The muscles of his jaw knotted, and his brows came down like thunder. She'd never seen him look so angry, and she quailed instinctively from him. Then he strode to the bedside table, and picked up Stuart's ring.

She gave a little cry of alarm, but he was already opening the window. He flung it out into the darkness with explosive force. She didn't even hear it land.

'Oh, Jan,' she sighed. 'That wasn't very clever. I'll never find it out there.'

'That's the general idea,' he said grimly.

'Stuart took *ages* choosing that ring,' she said. 'How am I going to tell him. . .?' But she felt laughter, her old enemy, starting to bubble up in her, even as she rebuked Jan. She tried to fight it down, but there was something about his action that made her heart soar like a bird. 'What am I supposed to tell him?' she demanded, smiling despite herself.

'Tell him Jan Breydel threw it out of the window.'

'You know I can't tell him that.' Geraldine reached up to the clasp of the gold rope he'd given her. 'And I can't wear this either, Jan. I can't accept such a sumptuous gift. Please take it back.'

'No. I bought it for you.' His anger faded. He reached out, and caught her wrists, stopping her from taking it off. 'Leave it on,' he said in a grainy voice. 'It looks so beautiful on you. And while you wear it, I can at least pretend. . .that you are mine.'

'Oh, Jan,' she said, responding emotionally, as always, to his moods, 'don't talk like that. Please!'

'Why not?' He drew her to him, and slid his arms around her waist. He smiled down into her eyes. 'Wouldn't you like to pretend the same thing, just for a while?'

'It sounds a very dangerous game.'

'I only like dangerous games. And you?'

'I used to. Not any more. I hate being hurt, Jan.'

'I'll never hurt you,' he whispered, imprisoning her in his arms as he bent down to touch each of her temples in turn with his lips. She shivered defencelessly. His kiss was so delicate, so intoxicatingly sweet. His breath was warm. She felt his mouth touch her brow, her cheeks, the sensitive, satin-soft skin beside her ears. He seemed to want to kiss every inch of her face, with tender care, as though kissing the most beautiful thing imaginable.

'I miss you so much,' he whispered as his mouth roamed over her fluttering eyelids. 'I need you at my side, constantly. . .'

'I miss you,' she couldn't help replying in a little moan. 'This house is a desert without you, Jan.'

He kissed the corners of her mouth in turn, then pressed his lips gently full on hers. 'Then you *do* care for me,' he said, and there was a husky note in his voice.

'Of course I care for you,' she said helplessly. 'That's what you set out to achieve, wasn't it?'

'You insist on seeing me as the great seducer, don't you?' He took her lower lip in his teeth, biting just hard enough to make her whimper. 'Perhaps that's what you really dream of, Geraldine. A man who'll leave you no choice, who'll just sweep you off your feet, and——'

Without warning, he lifted her easily in his arms. His strength was almost frightening at times. He carried her over to the bed, and laid her down.

'Oh, no,' she gasped. 'Jan, please. . .'

'"Jan, please",' he echoed mockingly. 'Is that an entreaty? Or an invitation?'

His mouth descended on hers before she could

answer. The gentle pressure of his lips forced her to yield. She felt his tongue caress the moist inner slopes of her lips, exploring inward with erotic provocation. And once again, she was falling into the bottomless chasm, lost in the power this man had over her.

His hands caressed her flanks, her thighs, sliding across the gentle curves of her body. He had a lingering, thrilling touch; he knew exactly how to set her aflame, to make her respond just as he wanted. Did she have no resistance against this onslaught? Was she becoming Jan Breydel's slave?

Yet she wanted this so much, wanted it with every fibre of her being. It was more than arousal; she had felt that once or twice before. It was a desire of utter union, to be melted into Jan's soul so that there was no longer any space between her and him.

His fingers were deft as they plucked the ribbons of her nightgown loose, and spread the filmy material aside, revealing the perfect curves of her breasts.

'No, Jan,' she gasped, 'please don't do this to me!'

He was kissing her throat, burying his face in the scented hollow where her collarbones met. She arched as his kisses grew more erotic, tracing the swelling curve of her breast, until she felt his mouth claim the erect peak of her nipple. She gasped at the almost cruel pressure of his teeth on the intensely sensitive flesh. She felt as though she were being sucked into a vortex, a spiral of desire that had no bottom, no end. . .

'You smell so wonderful, Geraldine,' he whispered raggedly, moving to her other breast. 'You smell like a whole garden of flowers in bloom. And your skin is like silk. . .warm, living silk. . .'

His tongue encircled the peak of her breast in a hungry caress, tracing ever inward, until he drew the aroused centre into his mouth, and she cried out aloud at the desire that surged through her body.

She felt as though her frame were dissolving from the waist down, all her strength melting into a languorous readiness. As the palm of his hand slid down her belly, caressing in gentle circles, she was unable to stop the treacherous response of her own limbs, enticing him on, inviting him, yearning for him. . .

'Tell me you're mine,' he commanded in a fierce whisper, his fingers sliding along her inner thigh. 'Tell me!'

'You know I am,' she moaned. She lifted her drugged lids, and looked into his face. He was smiling, but she could see the answering desire in his eyes, in the flare of nostrils. 'Jan, this is madness!'

'Then let go,' he advised, kissing her soft mouth. 'Let go, and forget sanity, my love.'

His fingers had discovered the height of her arousal. She felt a dizzy wave of ecstasy as his caress deepened, became unbearably intimate. No pleasure in her life had ever been as intense as this, as wickedly sweet. He was touching her soul, caressing places that no man had ever reached before. He was finding peaks and valleys of delight that she herself had never been aware of until this burning moment, this magical present.

She felt, through her passion, that everything in her life had been somehow leading towards this point, this union. That everything that had come before had just been a preparation for Jan. Her schooldays, her time at college, her work—all an elaborate process that had as its end nothing more than bringing here, to this moment.

She could feel the hard thrust of his own arousal against her, and she touched him gently there, hearing his gasp of passion as she traced the conspicuous outline of his body. . .

'With Jan one tends to lose one's head. . .he's very forceful. . . I'm sure you can imagine. . .' Lisa's words echoed derisively in her mind. God, what kind of fool was she being?

She felt the tears starting to her eyes. With a supreme effort, she caught his wrist. 'Please stop,' she implored.

He was too strong, and her own body was too treacherous. She brought her thighs together and trapped his hand there tightly.

'*Please*,' she said in a shaky voice that was unlike her own. 'No more.'

He saw the wet sheen in her eyes, and finally obeyed her. 'What are you crying for?' he asked urgently. 'What's the matter, Geraldine?'

'Nothing. My own stupidity, that's all.'

'You little goose. . .' He took her in his arms, not erotically this time, but comfortingly, and held her close as she got over her tears. They took a long time to subside. The other feelings, the feelings of aphrodisiac hunger that he had aroused in her, did not subside at all. Slowly, an ache of unfulfilment spread through her. Better that pain, she told herself, than the pleasure that would have led to a broken heart for her!

'Are you feeling better?' he asked.

'A little.' She put her palm on his chest as he leaned forward to kiss her. 'No, don't do that,' she said unsteadily. 'Let's just talk.'

'Talk?' he smiled. 'How very English. Very well. What shall we talk about? How about you and me?'

'No!' she said, drawing her nightdress closed. 'Ordinary things, small talk, anything. . .' Her fingers seemed too weak to fasten the ribbons again, and he reached out to do it for her. It was perilous ground, but she had to trust him.

'There,' he said. 'You're all buttoned up again.' They lay together on the bed, not touching, but the memory of their desire still smouldering between them. 'Delicious Geraldine has gone. Cool Miss Simpson from London has returned in her place. What shall we discuss, Miss Simpson?'

'Tell me how your week has been,' she invited.

'Without you? A black hole. And yours?'

'Oh, up and down. How is Lisa?'

'Fully recovered, I think. I haven't seen her, but she called me just as I was going out with a friend last night. We had a brief chat.'

'You're having a busy time, even for such a noted Don Juan,' she said wryly.

He laughed. 'Tell me something, Geraldine. Exactly

why are you so convinced that I'm such a seducer of women?'

'Aren't you? You've just given a pretty good impression of one.'

He touched her lips with his fingertip. '*Touché*. Very well, I'll rephrase that. Exactly why are you so convinced that I'm immoral?'

'Someone with eyes like yours,' she replied, 'just *has* to be immoral. The devil designed those eyes with only one purpose in mind—to get silly women into the bedroom.'

'That's not a very convincing reason,' he said gently.

'Oh, it is to me. You're just too beautiful to be moral, Jan.'

'I suppose I could take that as a sort of back-handed compliment,' he sighed.

'You've given me enough of those,' she replied. 'Do you want to know what the most truly wicked thing about you is?'

'I'd love to know the most wicked thing about me,' he said, amused.

'It's your ability to make me feel that there really is something special between us. That you aren't just a tom-cat on the make, but a sincere, loving suitor with only the most honourable intentions.'

He raised his dark eyebrows. 'Have I behaved dishonourably?'

'You've just tried to make love to me,' she pointed out.

'And before we're even engaged,' he said, clicking his tongue in mock-horror. 'Don't worry, Miss Simpson. I'm fully aware of your chaste condition. I wouldn't be so bold as to try and assail your virtue.'

'What *would* you have done, then?' she asked sceptically.

'Let me show you,' he purred, reaching for her again.

'Oh, no, please,' she said in genuine dismay. 'I wouldn't be able to stop you again. . .'

His eyes glinted. 'An excellent reason for going on,'

he said. 'But to get back to our discussion—don't you feel that perhaps there *is* something special between us? That I may not be just—what was your charming expression?—a tom-cat on the make, but a man who simply wants to show you his true feelings?'

'No, I don't, actually.'

'Doesn't this tell you anything?' he enquired gently, tugging at the heavy gold chain still looped around her throat.

Geraldine flushed. 'It's very beautiful, Jan. I know it must have cost you a lot of money. I've never possessed a piece of jewellery like it before, and I don't suppose I ever will again.'

'Not if you marry Stuart Horwood. That was the smallest diamond I've ever seen.'

'But I also know,' she went on, not rising to the bait, 'that you're a very rich man, and can afford to spend a little money to get your pleasures.'

'You little shrew,' he said quietly. 'You know how to make me angry!'

She drew her finger slowly down the line of his nose, studying the magnificent face intently, until she was touching the deeply carved lips. 'That's what I mean,' she said. 'You're so convincing that you probably even fool yourself. You actually believe that your intentions are honourable. . .until you get what you want, and then——'

'And then?'

'And then you get bored, and move on to the next Geraldine Simpson. Or more likely, the next Lisa Groenewald.'

He bit her finger hard enough to make her yelp. 'That hurt!'

'Good,' he said unrepentantly, and rose. 'Well, having failed to seduce you, I might as well take my tom-cat self off to bed. You're safe. Aren't you going to show me out?'

She rose, and was not surprised to find that her legs were almost too wobbly to support her. She walked with him to the door. There, he kissed her with great tenderness on the lips—such tenderness that she felt, with something like pain, that he might almost have meant every word. . .

'Goodnight,' he whispered. 'Dream of me.'

She closed the door and sagged against it, her eyes closing. God, the devastating effect he had on her! Safe? He was about as safe as a Bengal tiger who hadn't eaten for three days. And yet, why did her heart soar like this? Why did this mountain of happiness lift her up among the clouds, and make her head spin with joy?

She walked to the mirror, and looked at her own reflection, remembering the way he had held her in his arms. Her face was soft, vulnerable. So vulnerable that it was hard to understand how he hadn't managed to have his way with her.

She touched the gold rope around her neck. It was an exquisitely wrought thing, quite clearly the work of a truly gifted designer, and very far from the mass-produced article of ordinary jewellers' shops. God alone knew how much it had cost him. More than her salary for six months, she suspected. She'd never been given anything a fraction as precious as this. It was a truly dazzling gift. In jewellery, evidently, as in all things, Jan had spectacular taste. No doubt, she told herself with a bittersweet smile, he'd had plenty of practice buying jewellery for the ladies in his life! What on earth was Stuart going to say when he found out? What would he say when he learned his ring had been hurled out of the window?

Leave tomorrow to tomorrow, she sighed, taking her aching body to bed. She reached up to unfasten the rope. But her fingers would not obey. She couldn't bear to take it off.

You can't sleep in it, she told herself tiredly. You might choke.

'Then I'll die happy,' she said aloud, and slid between the sheets without taking it off.

She lay thinking of Jan, touching the smooth gold with her fingertips. And then exhaustion sealed her eyelids, and darkness crept in.

CHAPTER TEN

'You did *what*?' Stuart said in horror.

It was just before lunch the next day. They were in the gallery, where Stuart was packing up his photographic equipment.

'I lost it,' Geraldine repeated nervously. 'I'm so sorry, Stu. I can't believe I could have been so stupid. I went for a stroll in the garden, and it must have fallen out of my pocket——'

'My God, Geraldine! That was gross carelessness!'

'I've looked and looked. I've hunted for four hours.' That part of her story, at least, was true enough. 'But I can't find it anywhere. It must have dropped among the leaves. There are so many, with it being autumn. . .it's like looking for a needle in a haystack.'

And for all she knew, Jan might have hurled it clear over the garden wall, and into the canal. But she couldn't say that.

Stuart was glaring at her, as though still unable to believe what she was telling him. 'Do you have any idea what that ring cost me?' he demanded.

'I'm so sorry,' she repeated miserably.

'That was a *diamond*, in case you hadn't noticed.'

'I know, Stu.'

He took in a deep breath. 'Well, you're just going to have to keep looking,' he said grimly.

'I'll go back after lunch,' she sighed.

'You'll go back now! This is more important than lunch, Geraldine. Or have you lost all sense of proportion?'

'But, Stuart——'

'Somebody else might find it in the meantime.'

'Who?'

'A gardener, anybody with sharper eyes than you.

It's not even really yours! Whatever happens between us, that ring remains *my* property.'

'Does it?' she said, surprised out of her unhappiness.

'*I* paid for it,' he said in a thin voice. 'I would expect you to have the refinement of feeling to return it to me if our engagement was broken off. I could at least try and get back some of the hard-earned money I've wasted!'

She stared at him. She had an extraordinary feeling of seeing the man for the first time in her life.

He'd grown so familiar to her over the past three years, distinguished, consequential Stuart, with his wise grey eyes and silvering hair.

But suddenly, she was seeing someone else; a pretentious little man with a pot belly and a peevish voice. A shallow, vain little man, who looked at her with no affection in his eyes, and spoke to her with no warmth in his voice.

And realisation came suddenly that she had no feelings for him. *I don't love him*, she thought, almost absently. *I don't love him at all.*

'Well?' Stuart snapped at her. 'Don't just stand there like a dummy. Go back out into the garden, and keep looking until you find it.'

'No,' she said.

He gaped. 'What?'

'I said, no. I'm not going to look for that ring any more.' She was speaking quite calmly, despite her anger. 'I've decided that you're right. It *is* your ring. So *you* can go and look for it. And when you've found it, take it back to the jeweller you bought it from, and see if you can get your money back. I'm sure he'll be used to that particular request.'

She turned, and walked out of the gallery.

'Geraldine!' he called after her, his voice shrill with anger. 'This is intolerable behaviour!'

She paused at the door, and looked over her shoulder at him. 'A little hint, Stu—look at the far end of the garden. The *very* far end. I won't be at lunch. I'm going out.'

'You can't!'

'I've worked two weekends in a row,' she snapped. 'I'm not working this one.'

She walked out of the front door, slamming it hard behind her. She crossed the courtyard, and walked briskly into the street. Her blood was singing in her ears.

'*Condescending* little man,' she muttered to herself furiously. 'Vain, conceited, puffed-up, *rude* little man!'

She strode along, barely noticing her surroundings, until her cheeks were flushed, both with the emotion and with the energetic pace she had set herself. Panting slightly, she had to slow down.

She relaxed her taut neck muscles, and breathed deeply. In her anger, she hadn't even taken a purse with her. But she was damned if she was going back to that house until she was in a better mood. Where should she take herself? She looked round her at the charmingly quaint architecture of the old houses, and paused uncertainly at a street-corner.

Then she heard the rumble of a powerful engine behind her, and turned. The crimson Ferrari purred alongside her, and pulled to a halt. Jan got out, and leaned on the roof, his deep blue eyes smiling at her.

'Going somewhere?'

'Yes,' she said shortly, glowering at him.

'Where?'

'I don't know, yet. I haven't decided.'

He walked round, and opened the passenger door. 'Get in. When you've made your mind up, I'll take you there.'

'I just want to be alone!'

'Come on, Greta Garbo. Don't argue.'

She climbed reluctantly in, and settled herself into the white leather upholstery. Jan got behind the wheel, and turned to her. 'Where to?'

'I'm still deciding. How did you know where I'd gone?'

'I heard the door slam. Looked out of the window just in time to see you stalking into the street like a prima donna. I got in the car and followed. What happened?'

'It's all your fault, damn you,' she snapped.

'What is?'

'I had to tell Stuart I'd lost his ring. He was horrible to me.'

'Was he? Want me to go back and throw the little squirt into the canal?'

'Haven't you done enough damage for one weekend?' she retorted. 'Besides, I'm not going back home until I feel a great deal better.'

'No problem,' he smiled, putting the Ferrari into gear. 'If that's what you want, I'll take you to see something that will put you right.'

She sat in a sullen silence as he drove through the city. She could not tell whom she was angrier with, Jan or Stuart.

He parked the car a few minutes later, by the side of a canal. Across the canal stood a magnificent Gothic church, its steeple reaching up high into the sky. She felt her mood lift slightly.

'Is this it?'

'Yes. Come along.'

He held her hand as they crossed the worn stone bridge that led to the church. She lifted her gaze to the delicate flying buttresses, the mullioned windows above, and finally, to the spire that towered majestically over it all.

'It looks as though it's touching the sky,' she said in awe.

'It's one of the highest in Europe. Medieval builders believed in getting as close to heaven as they could. But what I really brought you here to see is inside.'

They entered the echoing, almost deserted church. She gazed up in reverence at the vaults that arched hundreds of feet over their heads. She had never been much interested in church architecture, graphic arts being her favourites; but this was one of the most awe-inspiring monuments she had ever been in.

Jan led her forward. 'This is the church of Notre Dame,' he told her. 'And there she is.'

Geraldine looked up. Standing in a curved alcove of black basalt was a life-size carving of the Virgin and Child. The white marble glowed against the black background. The carving was magnificent; the drapery of the robe falling in soft folds, the pose of the naked Child meltingly natural. But most beautiful of all was the serene face of the Virgin herself. She gazed modestly down, one lovely hand supporting the Child, the other holding a book in her lap.

The masterpiece was unmistakable.

'It's a Michelangelo,' she said quietly.

Jan nodded. 'One of the very few outside Italy. She was brought here around 1514, and she has sat there for nearly five hundred years. There isn't a greater work of art in all Bruges.'

Geraldine felt the tranquil radiance of the sculpture soak into her spirit, chasing out all her anger and pain. She gazed upwards, rapt.

Jan put an arm around her waist, and drew her close. 'I used to come here as a boy, and gaze up at her, just the way you're doing now. Tell me, don't you think she looks like you?'

'Like *me*?'

'Look. The same oval face. The same long nose, the same beautiful eyes and mouth. The same expression, calm and sweet.'

She was colouring. 'I'm not sure that isn't irreverent, Jan!'

'It isn't irreverent at all. I'm a religious man—in my own way. Michelangelo used a model for that statue, and I believe that model must have looked a lot like you.' He turned to her. 'I loved that statue as a boy. It brought me so much peace. Perhaps that's partly why I fell in love with you the moment I saw you.'

Her eyes filled with tears. 'Don't say that!'

'It's the truth.' He touched her cheek with a smile that made her trembling heart ache.

When she had looked her fill, they emerged into the autumn sunshine. 'Hungry?' he asked her.

'Ravenous,' she said, thinking of the meal she had missed.

'Come on. We'll have lunch, and then I'll show you something else Bruges is famous for.'

They ate in a charming little restaurant on one of the canals. Their table was in a bow window that hung just over the water, so that she could watch the snowy white swans gliding to and fro almost within touching distance.

She agreed to his choice of *carbonade flamande*, a rich beef stew that was one of Bruges's favourite dishes. It was delicious, washed down with the Bordeaux that Jan ordered.

It occurred to Geraldine to wonder what sort of lunch Stuart and Anna were having together. No doubt both would be making heavy weather of it. Stuart would be seething.

She didn't care. When she was with Jan, she didn't care about anything. He filled her soul with joy, and there was no room for anything else.

'Are you really so very rich?' she asked him, looking at him over the rim of her wine glass.

He laughed. 'I do a lot of business every year. My turnover is very big. But personally speaking, I'm not nearly as rich as many people I know. For example, I have a friend who inherited a hundred million pounds from his father. I don't have anything like that.'

'That's iniquitous!'

Jan shrugged. 'Good luck to him. If you don't have to work for it, so much the better.'

'But you worked for yours.'

'Very hard.' He smiled. 'I'm just getting to the stage in my life where I'm learning that there are more things in life than work. I'm learning to look beyond that, to the things that really count.'

'Like what?'

'Like you.' She buried her confusion in the wine. He was amused. 'I'm not very materialistic. I have all of the things I want. A yacht in the south of France. A good car. A nice house with a pretty garden.'

'A garden!' She thought of her own horticultural dreams. 'Is it big?'

'Not especially. Three or four acres.'

'Three or four *acres*,' she repeated wryly. So much for hollyhocks and a privet hedge in some suburban plot! 'Is it a modern house?'

'Very. It was designed for me by one of the most avant-garde architects in Belgium. It's—unusual. My friends thought I was crazy at the time. But I love it. And so, I hope, will you.'

'I doubt if I'll ever see it,' she said, looking down. 'I suppose you wanted to get as far away from your childhood memories as possible?'

'It was partly that, I suppose.'

'And do you still think the memories will go when you've sold the Bruges house?'

'I'm beginning not to care about those memories any more,' he smiled. 'They're one of the things that just don't seem important any more.' His eyes dropped to her throat. 'You're not wearing your chain?'

'Well. . .' she said. She unfastened the high collar of her blouse, and revealed the gold rope beneath. 'Cowardly, I know. But I couldn't bear to take it off, and I didn't dare let Stuart see it.' She grimaced. 'It was hard enough explaining how I'd lost his ring, without having to explain away *this* as well.'

'He'll find out sooner or later.'

'Yes.' She toyed with her wine glass, hesitating over her next words. 'I made a discovery this morning.'

'About Stuart?'

'About him, and about me. I suppose it should have come as a big shock to me, but somehow it didn't. I ought to be in floods of tears. But I'm not.'

'You've discovered that you don't love him,' Jan said in a roughened voice. 'Is that it?'

She didn't answer. She'd been stupid to bring it up. Just because she'd seen through Stuart Horwood, it didn't mean she was about to leap from the frying pan into the fire. She shrugged. 'Forget it. It was just something silly. I shouldn't have mentioned it.'

Jan was silent for a while. 'He tells me he's going back to London tomorrow?' he said at last.

Geraldine nodded. 'His work is finished. He has to get back to the auction house.'

'And you're staying on alone for a week or two?'

'Yes,' she confirmed, not meeting his eyes.

'That's a coincidence,' he said silkily. 'I was just thinking of taking a fortnight off work from Monday. We'll be able to spend some time together.'

She looked up. And as her eyes met his, she knew that she would not be able to resist Jan on her own. Stuart had been a feeble enough prop, God knew. But without him, her defences would simply crumble away. . .and Jan Breydel would do with her exactly as he chose!

Her mouth was dry as she tore her eyes away from the certainty in his.

'I look forward to that,' he purred. 'Let's go and do some shopping.' He turned, and signalled to the waiter for the bill.

'I'm not Lisa, you know,' she whispered, as Jan ordered the immense box of chocolates to be wrapped. 'I can't possibly eat all that lot. I'd end up as fat as a pig!'

'Chocolates are the natural food of lovers,' he smiled. 'Besides, they're one of the things we Belgians do best. There are over two thousand chocolate shops in the country—and it isn't a very big country. Did you know that every Belgian eats twenty-four pounds of chocolate each year?'

'I can well believe that,' Geraldine said wryly. The foremost *chocolatier* of the city was not a place for the weak-willed; the more than fifty kinds of bonbon on display constituted masterpieces in themselves.

Jan had obliged her to taste as many of them as she could manage. The wonderful flavours lingered on her tongue—cognac butter cream, pistachio praline, *crème fraîche*, Grenoble walnuts, the sharper flavours of crushed strawberries and coffee liqueur. . .had she eaten even one more bonbon, she was sure, she would have started feeling sick. 'I suppose the Belgians invented chocolate?' she teased him.

'No, the Aztecs did that. But it was a Belgian who invented the filled chocolate bonbon. A great step forward for humanity,' he added solemnly.

The box arrived back in front of them, sumptuously wrapped in silk ribbons and gold string. Jan paid, and led her out to the car.

'Now,' he promised, 'I'll show you another of the products Bruges is famous for.'

As Jan drove, she curled up in the seat beside him, revelling in the rich smell of the leather, and watched his aquiline profile. She had never felt so happy in her life. The brightness of his personality illuminated every dark corner, chasing away shadows and doubts. It was only when she was not with him, she realised, that the misgivings came to torment her. When she was with him, there was nothing but joy.

That, she told herself sarcastically, was no doubt exactly why he was so successful with women.

The next place he took her to was a sunny little square beside the river. A group of old ladies were sitting in the sun, working industriously at some handicraft on wooden benches. Many of them wore traditional head-scarves of a red polka-dot pattern, and Geraldine had the eerie impression that they had been there since the Middle Ages, at least.

As they approached, she realised that the handicraft they were producing was—what else?—lace.

'Bruges lace,' Jan confirmed. 'It's been the finest lace in Europe for hundreds of years.'

She stared in fascination at the intricate work. The threads were strung on little wooden bobbins, and some of the women seemed to be working with an astonishing number. She counted the bobbins on one bench.

'She's working with sixty bobbins,' she told Jan in astonishment.

'Not bad,' he smiled. 'But some of the best work is done with well over three hundred bobbins. It's called the *sorcière* stitch.'

Amazed by the deftness of the old ladies—not to mention their eyesight—Geraldine watched the wrinkled brown fingers flickering over the work. Like ancient spiders, she thought, spinning wonderful ornamental webs.

'Those designs are wonderful,' she sighed. The floral patterns had no doubt been handed down from mother to daughter over centuries. She ached to possess one of these marvels of feminine ingenuity; but she could only imagine how much this laborious work must cost. Far more, anyway, than her meagre salary would allow.

Jan led her into one of the ancient houses that lined the square. It turned out to be a small shop, in which several finished pieces of work were on display. Geraldine touched a set of lace doilies longingly. How her mother would have loved these. But she could see the price-tag, and a quick conversion into sterling told her that any such extravagance was out of the question.

Jan was speaking in Flemish to the shopkeeper. She smiled and nodded, and bustled off to the back of her shop. She reappeared a little while later with a large, flat box, which she opened reverently. She beckoned Geraldine to come and look.

Carefully wrapped in tissue paper was a large lace veil. Geraldine lifted it with gentle fingers. The pattern of poppy-flowers was exquisite, a gossamer wonder of tiny loops and whorls that looked as though it would fly away at a breath, and yet was surprisingly strong. She tried to guess at the hours upon hours of masterly work this garment had entailed, and was dumbfounded.

'It's a wonderful thing,' she told Jan. 'I've never seen anything like it.'

'It was made by this lady's mother, many years ago. The women of Bruges used to wear this sort of veil on their heads, to go to church on special days, like Christmas or Easter. Try it on.'

'Oh, no,' she said in protest, 'I couldn't.' But he was already looping it over her dark hair, and arranging the delicate folds to fall on either side of her oval face. He stepped back to admire the effect. 'You look like a bride,' he said in a soft voice. 'Do you like it?'

'It's stunning,' she sighed. 'Tell her I've never seen finer work than this.'

Jan nodded to the woman, and said something in Flemish. She beamed, and wrapped the shawl back in its tissue-paper. Then she started gift-wrapping the box.

'Jan, *no*,' she said urgently, suddenly realising what was afoot. 'Don't even think of it.'

'Why not?' he said, caressing her cheek affectionately with the backs of his knuckles.

'You can't spend money on me like this,' she exclaimed passionately. 'It's not right! Can't you see what an impossible position it puts me in?'

'No,' he said, 'I can't.'

'You may be rich, Jan,' she told him, 'but I'm not. I can't let you do this.'

He smiled. 'As I said before, you don't have any choice. Learn to accept graciously. Besides, you never know when you'll want to go to church next.'

Helplessly, she had to give way. But these fabulous gifts did not make her feel any happier. Where a more mercenary woman might have grasped at Jan's bounty with open hands, Geraldine was dismayed. These overwhelmingly beautiful tributes frightened her. They made her feel that she was steadily losing control over this relationship—if she'd ever had any control to start with, that was. . .

They got back as the autumn afternoon was closing in, and the warmth of the sun was going out of the air. She was in a blissful mood, as though the blood in her veins had been replaced with foaming champagne. That was what Jan Breydel did to her!

It was like coming down to earth with a thud to see Stuart Horwood's frozen expression awaiting her.

'I'd like to speak to you for a moment,' he said fatefully. 'That is, of course, if you can spare the time from your busy schedule.'

The heavy sarcasm made her heart sink. It showed Stuart was at his angriest.

He led her into the gallery, and closed the door emphatically behind them. He turned to her, his mouth compressed into a thin line.

'I imagine you already know what I'm about to say to you,' he said.

'Yes,' she agreed quietly. 'I suppose I do.'

'I'm not a man who makes many mistakes, Geraldine. My judgement is usually impeccable. But this time, I have been extremely imprudent. My engagement to you was a dreadful mistake. The best thing we can do, I think, is to consider the whole episode closed—for ever.'

'I agree,' she replied, in an even quieter voice. 'And I'm sorry, Stuart.'

'The fault is partly mine,' he said grimly. 'I over-estimated your maturity. And I underestimated the problems of your inexperience, your upbringing, and your background——'

'Stuart,' she said clearly, 'say what you like about me. But leave my background and upbringing out of it. All right?'

He made an effort to bite back his next words. 'All right,' he said at last, 'though I did have plenty to say on that score.'

'I can imagine. Let's just stick to you and me.'

'The plain and simple fact is that you do not come up to the expectations I would have of a wife. I am sorry to have to put it so bluntly. Perhaps my expectations were too high. My first marriage was, after an initial settling-in period, almost flawless. Nevertheless, I agree that I am a demanding man. I have decided to look for a more suitable woman. That means I can no longer consider you in a matrimonial light.'

'I understand.' She felt no pain, only an unspeakable relief, as though a vastly heavy weight had slid off her shoulders. She even felt that she was standing more upright, with her head held higher. She met his eyes directly. 'What about work, Stuart? I imagine you won't want me to stay in the firm after this?'

He looked away, refusing to meet her dark eyes. 'I'm not about to suspend your contract,' he said, picking his words with care. 'That would lay me open to a charge——'

'I know. Of unfair dismissal.'

'Perhaps even sexual discrimination,' he agreed. 'But let's say this—if you had the delicacy of feeling to seek other employment, I would appreciate it. To the extent that you could count on a good testimonial from me.'

'Thank you, Stuart,' she said with faint irony. 'I appreciate that.'

'I pride myself on being a fair man,' he sniffed. 'You will, of course, remain on here and finish cataloguing the drawings and prints. But you can consider this your last job. When you get back to London, you can start making enquiries about other employment. In the meantime, no doubt,' he sneered, 'you will enjoy being closeted with your hero, Jan Breydel. And that, I think, concludes this singularly unpleasant interview. Except that I shall want someone to help me carry the camera equipment to the ferry terminal tomorrow.'

'I'll come and help you,' she agreed.

'How kind of you to give up some of your precious weekend,' he said nastily.

'It's all over, Stuart,' she said mildly. 'You don't have to use that tone of voice any more.'

'All right,' he conceded, brushing some invisible specks of dust off his suit. 'We'll revert to a business relationship. That suits me fine.'

He walked out of the gallery, leaving her alone.

She stood looking round her at the works of art—the Van Goghs, the Monets, the Old Masters. Their tranquil beauty soaked into her, just as the beauty of the Madonna had soothed her this morning.

She was free. It was over. She was no longer engaged, and evidently soon to be no longer in gainful employment, either. No ties. No chains to bind her.

She wondered where she was going to find another job in these times. Her situation was not exactly an easy one. She ought to have been worried sick about her future.

But somehow it didn't matter. She was free!

She felt as though a cage door had been opened inside her, and a thousand white doves were soaring upwards, lifting her out of a dark place where she seemed to have been imprisoned for so long. . .

The joy made her laugh out loud.

Then, unaccountably, she started to cry.

There had been no way of hiding what had happened from Jan.

Those indigo eyes of his missed nothing, and his unmistakable knowledge of the break-up made their last supper together even harder to get through. Stuart and he discussed some details of the forthcoming sale, but the tension in the atmosphere weighed heavily on them all.

Feeling deeply depressed about the whole thing, Geraldine excused herself as soon after supper as was decent, and tried to find solace in sleep.

The next morning, at the ferry terminal at Zeebrugge, she and Stuart emerged from the taxi into a fine drizzle of rain. Appropriately grey weather, she thought, for a parting of this sort. They hustled the camera equipment into the terminal building, and headed for Embarkation. They did not talk much. He was in a subdued mood—and she was not relishing this moment, either.

At the gates, they paused, and faced one another. Their eyes met.

'Well,' Stuart said.

'Well,' she sighed. 'This is goodbye until next week.'

He nodded. 'No hard feelings, Geraldine?'

'No hard feelings,' she agreed, holding out her hand. He shook it briefly.

'I found the ring, by the way,' he said.

'Oh, I'm so glad!' she exclaimed. 'Where was it?'

'In the fountain,' he said, giving her an old-fashioned look. 'It took me ages to find it. How you came to lose it in there I will never know.'

She flushed slightly. It *would* have landed there. Stuart must have been seriously puzzled by that little detail. 'I'm glad you've got it back, anyway. Perhaps you can get a refund.'

'It wasn't really very expensive,' he said with an unexpected moment of candour. 'I might hang on to it.'

'You might need it again soon.'

'It'll come in handy,' he conceded. He looked at her briefly, then looked away. 'That man, Breydel. Don't be a fool over him, Geraldine. Just because you're on the rebound doesn't mean you have to do anything crazy.'

'I know,' she said.

'Good. You know, you never did say "yes" to me.'

'I beg your pardon?'

'The night I proposed to you in London—you didn't say "yes". I just rushed you into thinking you had agreed. You hadn't agreed, at all. You were just confused, and a little tipsy. Perhaps that's where the whole thing started to go wrong.'

'Perhaps,' she sighed.

'Another thing. I've been thinking over what we discussed yesterday. About you leaving Horwood & Littlejohn, I mean. Perhaps I was too harsh. After all, you *are* very good at your job. And I'm not sure where we'll find anyone of the same calibre to replace you in Prints and Drawings. So I think you should consider staying on.'

'I'm flattered,' she said regretfully. 'But on consideration, it really would be better for me to go. It would make both our lives a lot easier.'

'If that's the way you feel,' he said, clearly disappointed.

'I'm sure it's for the best. I'll bring the catalogue of the prints and drawings to you next week. But after that, perhaps it's better I don't come in to work any more.'

'Ah, well. You can take a month's notice. Where will you go next?'

'I'm not sure. Perhaps I should do something different for a while. I feel like a break.'

'Hmm. Well, good luck in whatever you do.'

'Thank you, Stu.' She was pleased that their parting was turning out so amicably.

The echoing public address system interrupted their conversation, instructing all ferry passengers to board at once.

'That's me,' he said. 'Goodbye, Geraldine.'

She kissed his cheek. 'Goodbye Stuart. See you soon.'

She watched him move through the gates, a sober little man with a sober little face. She was glad she hadn't ended up hating Stuart Horwood. It had just been, as he had said, a terrible mistake. Well, that mistake had been put right, now.

And don't make any more mistakes, she told herself, hunting in vain for a taxi in the drizzle outside. Remember—out of the frying-pan, but most definitely *not* into the fire!

Anna clucked indignantly at her soaked condition when she got home at noon.

'You'll catch your death of cold,' she said in the snappish tone that Geraldine had come to know was actually a sign of affection. 'Get those wet things off while I run you a hot bath.'

She obeyed, and was soon luxuriating in the steaming water. She had a delicious feeling inside her, a childhood feeling of excitement and contentment all at once. A phase of her life had ended. But on the other hand, that meant a new phase of her life was just beginning.

She couldn't help looking forward to the delight with which her parents and her two brothers would greet the news that she was no longer engaged to Stuart Horwood!

And even the prospect of job-hunting in a very difficult market could not douse her good spirits.

She soaped her smooth limbs with the fragrant Belgian soap she had found so delicious. With Stuart's departure, she felt that an oppressive presence in her life had lifted for ever. . .

When she had dried herself, and changed into warm, dry clothes, Anna brought a cup of tea to her bedroom.

'Lunch will be ready in a little while,' she said. 'Here's something to keep you warm in the meantime.'

'I'm as warm as toast already,' she smiled. 'But thanks.'

She noticed that Anna had brought a cup for herself, so they sat beside the crackling fire in amicable companionship.

'I can't say I'm sorry to see Stuart Horwood leave this house,' Anna said with brutal frankness. 'He was a most uncongenial man. And I shall never forgive him for being the agent of breaking up Cornelius's collection.'

Geraldine smiled. 'That's a little unfair. It was Jan's decision to sell up. Stuart was only doing his job. So was I. You forgive me, don't you?'

'Of course I do, Geraldine.'

'There you are—that proves you're being unfair.'

'Who said I was a fair person?' the old lady retorted. She sipped her tea thoughtfully. 'Mind you, Jan has been saying some odd things lately. Almost as though he were having second thoughts about the sale.'

'I've noticed that, too,' Geraldine said. 'But I didn't want to get my hopes up. Anyway, it's a little late for second thoughts, isn't it? Everything's practically settled.'

'It's never too late,' Anna said enigmatically. 'Not where Jan is concerned.'

'Well, I'd be absolutely delighted if Jan changed his mind. But Stuart would go mad.'

Anna snorted, as if to say, *who cares?* 'So you and he have broken off the engagement?'

'It's a hard job keeping secrets in this house,' Geraldine said wryly. 'But yes, we have.'

'Took you long enough to see the light,' Anna rejoined. 'And are you still. . .what was your word? *Obsessed* with my cousin?'

Geraldine swallowed. 'I should never have said that. It was a stupid thing to tell you.'

'It did not seem stupid at the time.'

'I was just a bit overwrought, what with Lisa's miscarriage——' She broke off in dismay, and laid her hand over her mouth, her eyes meeting Anna's guiltily.

Anna smiled drily. 'Oh, don't worry. You haven't betrayed a secret. I'm fully aware of the real nature of Lisa Groenewald's "illness".'

'Oh. . . I wasn't sure. I suppose not much that happens in this house escapes your notice. I suppose you also know she brought it on herself? She might have made herself a lot sicker than she did. She wasn't very clever.'

'Lisa has always been a stupid little creature. This time she's been even stupider than usual. She ought to be in a home for the incurably irresponsible.'

'Well, you can hardly free Jan from blame,' Geraldine couldn't help retorting.

'Jan?' The silvery eyes were like chips of ice. 'Why should Jan be to blame?'

'Well, it *was* his baby. You can't blame Lisa for everything.'

'*Jan's* baby?' Anna looked astounded. 'But of course it was not Jan's baby!'

Geraldine felt cold. 'But she told me—she told me he was the father!'

'She told you a pack of lies, in that case. And you were a fool to believe her, Geraldine.'

'She was absolutely specific!'

Anna's aquiline face was arctic. 'Jan is like an elder

brother to that little moppet. There has never been the slightest hint of anything else.'

'But then—why in God's name would she say such a thing?'

Anna put her teacup down, and folded her hands. 'Lisa Groenewald has been having a love-affair with a prominent Belgian politician for some months,' she said calmly. 'A *very* prominent politician. Who also happens to be very much married. Typical of Lisa, of course. Belgium is not a big country, and the scandal could have been very damaging indeed. But she did not care. And, obviously, she did not care enough to take precautions, either.'

Geraldine felt light-headed. 'Then it really wasn't Jan's?'

'Of course not. I'm astonished you could ever have thought that.'

Remorse tortured her. 'She told me it was Jan's! She even told the doctor!'

'Did she?' Anna's eyes glittered with disapproval. 'I can't say that's untypical, either. She is the most selfish person I have ever met. But I suppose she could hardly admit that the father was a man whose face appears practically every night on national television, either. And Jan has always been her white knight. Slandering his name would mean nothing to her, as long as she got out of hot water in the process. Let me tell you something about Lisa Groenewald, Geraldine. She has been running to Jan for help ever since she was in rompers. First it was bee-stings and scratched knees. Then teenage escapades that brought the police knocking on her parents' door. Later still, love-affairs that went wrong, gambling debts, even a drugs charge. And he, like the soft-hearted fool he is, always bails her out. This is only the last in a long, long line of scrapes, that he's helped her get out of—usually at considerable cost to himself.'

Geraldine wondered if she was going to faint. She put the teacup down with shaking fingers, knowing it would fall and break if she did not do so. 'God, I feel so awful. I—I was so convinced!'

'Is that what has been troubling you? The thought that Jan had made Lisa pregnant?'

'It wouldn't have been so terrible in itself,' she gulped, staring at Anna with haunted eyes. 'I'm not a prude. I know accidents happen. But when he tried to convince me he was serious about me—and I thought he was still having an affair with Lisa——'

Unexpectedly, Anna's fierce expression softened. 'I see. That must have been very painful for you.'

'I've been in hell!' she replied.

'Well, you're not in hell any more. Are you?'

'I can hardly believe it!'

'You think I'm trying to whitewash my cousin's character? I'll give you Lisa's number in Brussels. You can call her yourself, and get the true story.'

'I don't want to——'

'But you must,' Anna said calmly. 'It is the most important thing in your life. Or am I wrong?'

Geraldine took a shaky breath, and met the silvery eyes of the old lady. 'No,' she said unsteadily. 'You're not wrong, Anna. It is the most important thing in my life.'

She found Jan in the gallery, later on. He was sitting staring at the paintings arrayed all around, his chin in one hand.

His face lit up as she came in.

'Geraldine. . .' He rose and took her in his arms. This time, instead of flinching away from his kiss, as she so often, did, she raised her mouth eagerly to his. For a moment he looked surprised. Then their lips met with soft tenderness. He held her close. She closed her eyes, and clung around Jan's neck as the kiss deepened into that wonderful vortex that had no end. And for once, his power did not terrify her. It exalted her, made her seem to burst with joy.

She knew again, with even more certainty, that it was more than just sex, more than desire. It was a touching of souls. It was the love she had dreamed of for all those years. . .

She could tell, by the way his muscular body pressed to hers, that he felt it, too. And when they at last drew apart, he stared into her face with eyes that were blurred with passion.

'That's the first time you've kissed me like a lover,' he said softly. 'Is it because Stuart Horwood is out of your life?'

'No. Stuart was irrelevant.' She reached up, and touched his face. 'I've just had a conversation with your friend, Lisa Groenewald. She told me the truth about her pregnancy.'

'Ah,' he smiled. 'And that made a difference?'

'Oh, you fool,' she said, shaking her head. 'Of course it made a difference. All the difference in the world. When exactly would you have told me?'

'Soon. Within the next few days.'

'So you'd have left me in misery for days longer?'

He laughed, and kissed her yielding mouth with intense sensitivity. 'I was rather hoping you'd somehow find out on your own. I don't like to break a confidence.'

'A *confidence*!' she snorted. 'How could you let that wretched girl burden you with such a horrible accusation? I know she's like a little sister to you, but really, Jan. . .'

'Well, it was all rather thrust upon me. I knew who the father was, of course. She told you?'

'Yes.'

'Then you know what sort of scandal could have erupted. It would have brought shame on the whole country. So when Lisa told the doctor that lie, I was more or less forced into complicity. I'll never forget that look in your eyes! It cut me to the bone. I was cursing myself for ever having dreamed up that crazy scheme of bringing Lisa here to make you jealous. . . I might have known it would end up a disaster. I really ought to have known better. And there was no way I could explain, not at the time. Naturally, I gave Lisa hell about it afterwards. Not that giving Lisa hell about anything ever did any good.'

'She sounds an awful person. Why do you bother with her.'

He sighed, drawing her close to him. 'You didn't know Lisa as a little girl. She was so sweet-natured and helpless. I'd longed for brothers and sisters as a boy, and she filled a place in my heart for a while. She was an enchanting little girl, really she was. It was only later, when she grew up, that she turned into something of a monster.'

'I don't know whether to laugh or cry,' she said in a trembling voice. 'Well, at least I know how loyal you can be. . .and that gives me something to hold on to for the future.'

'What future?'

'Our future together,' she said, looking up at him.

He saw the look on her face. 'Does that mean you're not going to put up a fight any more?' he asked softly.

'Not unless you want me to,' she smiled.

'No,' he said, sounding a little breathless. 'I don't want you to.'

'I'm ready,' she told him simply. 'After I'd finished speaking to Lisa, I realised that. I don't know what the future holds for me with you. If you just want me to be your lover for a while, then that's what I'll be, and I'll take the pain of you leaving me when it comes. If you want something more serious and lasting, then I'll be ready for that, too. Whatever you want, Jan, I'm ready for it. I've never loved anyone the way I love you. I simply can't imagine living without you any more.' She took an unsteady breath. 'You've got what you wanted, Jan. You've made me fall in love with you. Are you pleased with yourself?'

He took her hand, and laid it over his heart. 'There's your answer,' he said quietly. She felt the pounding beat of his emotions, and her knees went weak. 'Oh, Jan. . .'

'I adore you, Geraldine. I've loved you almost from the first moment. I didn't need time to make my mind up. When you've waited for something all your life, you recognise it instantly when it comes. I don't know why you were so convinced I was not serious.'

'It was too wonderful to be true! It frightened me, Jan, and that's the truth. I was almost glad to have that lie of Lisa's to hold on to. It protected me from my own emotions!'

He drew her close. 'I know that fear. I felt it too, at first. Fear at the way your face haunted me, at the way your gentle ways and sweet voice wound themselves around the very fibres of my soul. . .' He sealed the words with a kiss. Then he went on, 'But you asked me a question just now. Whether I wanted you for a brief love-affair, or for something more permanent. From the very start, my love, I've known that there was one role I wanted you to fill in my life. One, and only one. I want you to be my wife, Geraldine.'

She closed her eyes, unable to speak.

He held her for a long while, caressing her cloudy, dark hair with gentle fingers. 'You haven't answered me,' he said at last. 'Will you marry me, my darling? Do you want me to get down on one knee?'

'No,' she whispered.

'No? You won't marry me?'

'No, I don't want you to go down on your knee. As for marrying you. . .'

Her lips gave him her answer in a kiss that was both delicious surrender and glorious possession. Not even in her wildest dreams had she imagined this happiness, this joy. Now, as she clung to him, overwhelmed by his strength, his desire, she knew that she was complete. There was nothing else in the world for her—only to be Jan's wife, and to bear his children when the time came. . .

An eternity later, their kiss ended, and they looked into each others' eyes. 'You can't go back to England,' he said huskily.

'I don't really have to,' she replied blissfully. 'Stuart's given me the sack.'

'How thoughtful of him,' Jan smiled. 'What a nice

man your ex-fiancé is. I'll have to refund him the cost of his ring.'

'No, he managed to find it in the end. It had fallen in the fountain. Don't you think that's significant?' she said, snuggling close to Jan. 'That fountain always seemed to symbolise you for me. A source of life, a source of joy and beauty. . .when you came into my life, the fountain that had dried up started to flow again. I'm sorry I was so ungrateful for that miracle at first. I was so terribly confused. . .'

Jan's kiss was a deep caress that quenched her thirst even as it made her yearn for more.

'So much has happened in such a short time,' he said. 'These past few weeks have been so overwhelmingly important in my life. It feels as though everything that came before just doesn't matter any more. As though it was all a black and white film that has suddenly exploded into glorious Technicolor!'

'It's only been a couple of weeks,' she smiled. His face blurred in her vision. 'I love you, Jan.'

'I love you, Geraldine. I'll love you all my life.' He drew her into his arms, into the heaven she'd longed for. 'For always.'

'I've decided not to sell the collection,' he said the next day, as they walked through the dappled sunlight under the trees, their arms wrapped around each others' waists.

'Jan! Why not?'

'You and Anna are right. The house and the paintings *are* part of my life. I can't just cut that part of me away. And I owe it to Anna and to Cornelius's memory to keep it all together.'

'I'm absolutely thrilled,' she exclaimed, looking up at him. 'But Stuart is going to have a fit! All that time spent cataloguing. . .'

'He did a good job. Essential preparation for the museum I'm going to set up.'

'Museum?' she blinked.

'Yes. I'm going to have the house restored and

turned into an art gallery. It shouldn't take too long to organise. I thought of calling it the Cornelius Breydel Foundation.'

They stopped, and she kissed him passionately on the mouth. 'How wonderful! Anna will be overjoyed.'

'I envisage making her chief consultant, of course. Nobody knows the collection better than she does. But she doesn't have the strength to supervise the arrangements for turning the house into a museum.' His indigo eyes met hers with a glint. 'I rather thought you might take that job over.'

'Me?' she gasped. 'Jan, I'm far too young and inexperienced for such a responsibility!'

'I know that you are perfectly capable. Besides, it will keep you out of harm's way until our wedding-day.' He smiled. 'I can't have you sitting around being idle while the fairies stitch your bridal gown. You might meet a man you liked more.'

'Oh, Jan,' she laughed, 'I'll never meet a man who even comes up to your knees in stature!'

'Your eyes are sparkling with excitement,' he said, leading her to the water's edge. 'I take it you like the idea?'

'I love it all,' she sighed tremulously. 'The museum, our marriage, our future together—and, most of all, I love *you*, Jan Breydel.'

'As for Stuart,' he went on, 'I've wired him a cheque this morning, together with an explanation. I think I've been liberal. The amount ought to more than cover his time and work here.'

'If *you* think you've been liberal,' she smiled, 'you've probably given him five times what was necessary. You're so generous, Jan!'

'Ah, but then, life has been so generous to me. It has given me you, Geraldine. It has crowned me with the greatest happiness any man can have—the love of a perfect wife.'

'I don't know if I'm going to be a perfect wife,' she said, choked by emotion. 'But I'll try, Jan. I'll try with all my heart.'

They stopped at the edge of the lake, and looked out across the water. The rains of yesterday had blown away, and sunlight danced like diamonds on the calm water. A pair of magnificent white swans drifted by, their graceful necks arched in unison.

This was where it had all begun—beside the lake of love, the Minnewater. Here, where the lovers of Bruges had come for centuries, their own love had taken root and begun to blossom.

'They mate for life, you know,' Jan said, his eyes on the white swans.

'So do I,' she smiled, drawing close to him.

'So do I,' he echoed.

And as their lips met in a kiss, Geraldine knew that her happiness was only just beginning.

BRUGES—'the Venice of the North'

Whether you're looking to spend a honeymoon, or a short break with that special person, Bruges is the perfect city for lovers.

Bruges was once an international trading centre, and that tradition lives on in its charming and virtually unspoilt streets. Bruges can certainly claim to be the prettiest city in Belgium—and the most romantic: visitors can sightsee by taking a cruise along tree-lined canals (crossed by fifty bridges), take a leisurely ride through the picturesque streets, or—if they're feeling more energetic—hire a bicycle.

Famous landmarks include the main square (**Markt**), with its magnificent thirteenth-century covered market (**Halle**) and the Belfry (**Belfort**); also the Law Courts (**Gerechtshof**) and the Green Quay (**Groene Rei**) where there are pretty gardens bordering the canal, that is crossed by hump-backed bridges from which you can see the Cathedral of Our Lady (**Onze Lieve Vrouwekerk**). The **Gruuthuse Palace** once housed the Dukes of Burgundy, while the **Groeninge** and **St John's Hospital** museums are still homes to masterpieces by famous painters.

THE ROMANTIC PAST. . .

Bruges was so attractive to the King of France, Philip the Fair, that he took it in 1301 from the Count of Flanders. When Philip arrived to claim his city, the ladies of Bruges were dressed so elegantly to greet him that his wife threw a jealous tantrum!

In the fifteenth century, the Flemish School of Art thrived on the beauty of Bruges, where famous artists such as Jan van Eyck, Hans Memling and Hugo van der Goes found inspiration.

In 1477, a statue of a little white bear named Beertje van de Loge was placed in the façade of the **Pooters Lodge** (Burghers' Hall). Beertje is still there today, standing on his hind legs and holding Bruges' coat of arms in his paws. The people of Bruges carry on the tradition of dressing Beertje in various costumes; it's said that his white fur looks best against a long red army cloak with gold fastenings!

THE ROMANTIC PRESENT—pastimes for lovers. . .

Bruges is a city for strolling and shopping in. Lovers may visit the flea markets on the **Dijver** on Saturdays and Sundays to uncover treasures, or perhaps they prefer to watch local artists paint in the open air. A beautiful sound to listen out for is the chiming of the forty-seven bells of the Bruges Carillon in the **Belfort**, which of course stands above the covered markets in the main square.

However, for many, the highlight of their trip to Bruges will be seeing how the city's lace-making tradition still continues; you can watch lace being made and buy it to take home. In the **Balstraat**, you will find the lace workshops, and the Junior Lace School where you can see children being taught this ancient skill.

For lovers of food, Bruges is where the desires of heart and stomach meet, because the city is famous for its delicious **pralines**—custom-made, filled chocolates; check out the **Steenstraat** for some of the best. There are also many canal-side restaurants in which to spend a candle-lit evening dining on the speciality dishes of the area: ***waterzooi*** is a variety of fish prepared with *bouillabaisse* and herbs; ***Gentse hotpot*** is a casserole containing all sorts of meats and local vegetables; ***Carbonades Flamandes*** is a type of sweet goulash.

However, no lovers' trip to Bruges is complete unless they have visited the **Minnewater**, the 'Lake of Love'. Once the heart of the harbour and a dock for commercial barges, the Minnewater has been transformed into a romantic spot where those in love can walk by the water and feed the famous white swans.

DID YOU KNOW THAT:

⋆ the brewing of Belgian **beer** is as much an art as, say, French wine-making; the average Belgian drinks 150 litres of beer a year, which is three times as much as the average Frenchman!

⋆ the currency of Belgium is the **franc**

⋆ the Belgians are the second greatest consumers of **chocolate** in Europe—only the British eat more!

⋆ a favourite Belgian sport is **sand-sailing**; when a strong wind blows off the North Sea, it's possible to travel along the beach at a terrific speed.

⋆ the Belgians have three official **languages**: French, Dutch and German; most are French or Flemish (Dutch) speaking.

⋆ when a Belgian says '*Je t'aime*', or '*Ek het jou lijf*', he means 'I love you'!

Travel across Europe in 1994 with Harlequin Presents and...

As you travel across Europe in 1994, visiting your favorite countries with your favorite authors, don't forget to collect four proofs of purchase to redeem for an appealing photo album. This photo album can hold over fifty 4" × 6" pictures of your travels and will be a precious keepsake in the years to come!

One proof of purchase can be found in the back pages of each POSTCARDS FROM EUROPE title...one every month until December 1994.

To receive your gift, please fill out the information below and mail four (4) original proof-of-purchase coupons from any Harlequin Presents POSTCARDS FROM EUROPE title plus $3.00 for postage and handling (check or money order—do not send cash), payable to Harlequin Books, to: IN THE U.S.: P.O. Box 9048, Buffalo, NY, 14269-9048; IN CANADA: P.O. Box 623, Fort Erie, Ontario, L2A 5X3.

Requests must be received by January 31, 1995.
Please allow 4–6 weeks after receipt of order for delivery.

POSTCARDS
HARLEQUIN PRESENTS®
FROM EUROPE

Name: ______________________
Address: ______________________
____
____
City: ______________________
State/Province: ______________________
Zip/Postal Code: ______________________
Account No: ______________________
ONE PROOF OF PURCHASE

077 KBY

INDULGE A LITTLE 6947 SWEEPSTAKES
NO PURCHASE NECESSARY

HERE'S HOW THE SWEEPSTAKES WORKS:
The Harlequin Reader Service shipments for January, February and March 1994 will contain, respectively, coupons for entry into three prize drawings: a trip for two to San Francisco, an Alaskan cruise for two and a trip for two to Hawaii. To be eligible for any drawing using an Entry Coupon, simply complete and mail according to directions.

There is no obligation to continue as a Reader Service subscriber to enter and be eligible for any prize drawing. You may also enter any drawing by hand printing your name and address on a 3" x 5" card and the destination of the prize you wish that entry to be considered for (i.e., San Francisco trip, Alaskan cruise or Hawaiian trip). Send your 3" x 5" entries to: Indulge a Little 6947 Sweepstakes, c/o Prize Destination you wish that entry to be considered for, P.O. Box 1315, Buffalo, NY 14269-1315, U.S.A. or Indulge a Little 6947 Sweepstakes, P.O. Box 610, Fort Erie, Ontario L2A 5X3, Canada.

To be eligible for the San Francisco trip, entries must be received by 4/30/94; for the Alaskan cruise, 5/31/94; and the Hawaiian trip, 6/30/94. No responsibility is assumed for lost, late or misdirected mail. Sweepstakes open to residents of the U.S. (except Puerto Rico) and Canada, 18 years of age or older. All applicable laws and regulations apply. Sweepstakes void wherever prohibited.

For a copy of the Official Rules, send a self-addressed, stamped envelope (WA residents need not affix return postage) to: Indulge a Little 6947 Rules, P.O. Box 4631, Blair, NE 68009, U.S.A.

INDR93

INDULGE A LITTLE 6947 SWEEPSTAKES
NO PURCHASE NECESSARY

HERE'S HOW THE SWEEPSTAKES WORKS:
The Harlequin Reader Service shipments for January, February and March 1994 will contain, respectively, coupons for entry into three prize drawings: a trip for two to San Francisco, an Alaskan cruise for two and a trip for two to Hawaii. To be eligible for any drawing using an Entry Coupon, simply complete and mail according to directions.

There is no obligation to continue as a Reader Service subscriber to enter and be eligible for any prize drawing. You may also enter any drawing by hand printing your name and address on a 3" x 5" card and the destination of the prize you wish that entry to be considered for (i.e., San Francisco trip, Alaskan cruise or Hawaiian trip). Send your 3" x 5" entries to: Indulge a Little 6947 Sweepstakes, c/o Prize Destination you wish that entry to be considered for, P.O. Box 1315, Buffalo, NY 14269-1315, U.S.A. or Indulge a Little 6947 Sweepstakes, P.O. Box 610, Fort Erie, Ontario L2A 5X3, Canada.

To be eligible for the San Francisco trip, entries must be received by 4/30/94; for the Alaskan cruise, 5/31/94; and the Hawaiian trip, 6/30/94. No responsibility is assumed for lost, late or misdirected mail. Sweepstakes open to residents of the U.S. (except Puerto Rico) and Canada, 18 years of age or older. All applicable laws and regulations apply. Sweepstakes void wherever prohibited.

For a copy of the Official Rules, send a self-addressed, stamped envelope (WA residents need not affix return postage) to: Indulge a Little 6947 Rules, P.O. Box 4631, Blair, NE 68009, U.S.A.

INDR93

INDULGE A LITTLE
SWEEPSTAKES

OFFICIAL ENTRY COUPON

This entry must be received by: APRIL 30, 1994
This month's winner will be notified by: MAY 15, 1994
Trip must be taken between: JUNE 30, 1994-JUNE 30, 1995

YES, I want to win the San Francisco vacation for two. I understand that the prize includes round-trip airfare, first-class hotel, rental car and pocket money as revealed on the "wallet" scratch-off card.

Name ______________________________

Address ____________________ Apt. __________

City ______________________________

State/Prov. ______________ Zip/Postal Code ______________

Daytime phone number ______________________________
(Area Code)

Account # ______________________________

Return entries with invoice in envelope provided. Each book in this shipment has two entry coupons—and the more coupons you enter, the better your chances of winning!

 MONTH1

INDULGE A LITTLE
SWEEPSTAKES

OFFICIAL ENTRY COUPON

This entry must be received by: APRIL 30, 1994
This month's winner will be notified by: MAY 15, 1994
Trip must be taken between: JUNE 30, 1994-JUNE 30, 1995

YES, I want to win the San Francisco vacation for two. I understand that the prize includes round-trip airfare, first-class hotel, rental car and pocket money as revealed on the "wallet" scratch-off card.

Name ______________________________

Address ____________________ Apt. __________

City ______________________________

State/Prov. ______________ Zip/Postal Code ______________

Daytime phone number ______________________________
(Area Code)

Account # ______________________________

Return entries with invoice in envelope provided. Each book in this shipment has two entry coupons—and the more coupons you enter, the better your chances of winning!

© 1993 HARLEQUIN ENTERPRISES LTD. MONTH1